THE SHORT
VE.

A.

Thank you for reading. If you enjoy this book, please leave a review.

Copyright © 2016 by A. S. Burt
Interior design by Pronoun

ISBN: 9781980934165

TABLE OF CONTENTS

Prologue

Ultimately, it had all been for nothing.

Hundreds of years of progress, expansion, technological breakthroughs... And now it came to this. The last space fleet orbited a violent star and had nowhere left to run. It consisted mostly of mining vessels and ragtag survival lifeboats, and each one was now battered. Many were broken. The fierce glow of the nearby celestial body rolled across the hulls of all the damaged ships, its stellar energy forcing the cooling systems into overdrive. Those systems, and the air regulation, were some of the only ones that still worked. Together, this flotilla of space craft had limped here, inch by inch, gathering around the blazing light of an impending supernova.

Wren Evans lived in the walls. Once, she had been human. But after several injuries, each one featuring a marked increase in severity, her mind had been uploaded into the ship's systems. Her body died, but she lived on. She was the first of her kind.

In the medical bay, the remnants of humanity—real humanity, with physical bodies and all that entails—fidgeted nervously as they awaited their fate. Wren scanned their vitals remotely and detected high stress levels in one hundred percent of them. After all they had been through, that was hardly surprising. Some of them were old enough to remember the meteor strike on Ark Gamma, the civil conflicts, and even the rogue star itself. Not to mention the recent and bloody final war.

Wren still had her personality, or at the very least, was programmed to think so. She scanned the archive of human history, examining the key events and milestones that had brought them to this moment. They had never come quite this close to extinction before. Only 73 humans left. Certainly not enough to win the fight against the-

A sudden influx of information rushed through her systems like a wave, interrupting her train of thought; Explosive decompression in the botanical gardens. Pointdash Nine had subsequently, within a fraction of a second, closed the doors and vented all the compartments of the Terraship Adam.

Pointdash Nine was perhaps the closest thing Wren had to a soul mate. Naturally, that means they hated each other. He was a true AI, originally programmed into a synthetic body, but he had long since uploaded himself into the network that pinged back and forth between the various craft that made up the fleet.

Wren opened a communications channel with him immediately.

"That was my ship."

She was talking about the Adam, of which she was previously the Captain.

"Receipt acknowledged. The target was a calculated risk of sixty-two-point-four percent, and the cargo deemed low priority."

Wren Evans was forced to admit, if only to herself, that Pointdash Nine had done the right thing. Her neural relays fired expeditiously, processing the incoming information and deducing that his maths was correct near instantaneously. So far, in her brief time as an uploaded human consciousness, he had always been right. But she liked to check.

The last vestiges of his people were still on board too, roaming the corridors of the fleet in search of combat. There was a truce between humans and robots, given the circumstances. An alien threat that nobody had seen coming. Pointdash was ruthless, calculated, and disconcertingly insightful. But he was the only other sentient being who had any idea what it *felt* like to be Wren.

There were plenty of significant differences between man and machine. Changes that Wren had to adapt to, now that she was no longer a corporeal creature. The expanded capacity for knowledge was the most obvious, but the abundance of time with which she found herself was another. She could consider everything she needed to, and have whole conversations with Pointdash Nine, all within milliseconds. One other key advantage was that she could relive any past events she recalled, and evoke any feeling she wanted from a distant memory.

That ability to reflect on her own extended life span had taught her a lot... Childhood memories of her father, the rainy days in the military academy in the halcyon days of terra firma, even her life on the Adam itself, and subsequent death—it had all been processed, her entire life experience condensed and assimilated in order to reach this decision. Her ultimate command. Her conclusion was simple enough in theory: Pointdash Nine and herself had to put aside their differences. Time had proven to be the most persistent villain, and no physical form was able to resist it. If any one of them could get out of this world alive, they would have to transcend.

Kolton was an old man, even by modern genetic standards. That was the most surprising thing about him, and the most notable, because truly old men were not a common sight. Not any more. His grey medical jacket covered his paunchy torso but his face had enough furrows to make it obvious, and the chiffon white hair completed the picture. But Kolton had always found a way, and it was that particular trait which made him the most important man in the Universe. As humanity had stumbled along the path to this moment, there were heavy losses, but Kolton and his staff in the science division had found a way to keep people going. It was his invention that allowed Wren to persist in her current form. His genius would be the basis for her plan. Together, they were going to make a new species.

Pointdash Nine scanned the information Wren transmitted. Her reasoning was undeniable, so he agreed to her plan. Together, they brought up images of themselves on the holographic projectors in the medbay. They could have projected any image they wanted, but both opted for their former selves.

For Pointdash, that meant a sleek curved bipedal body with a metallic racing green finish, surrounding a central optical sensor on the chest. His arms had some visible tubing, a deliberate design flourish rather than a functional necessity, leading to his strangely human hands. The chamois leather he was built with was supposed to make his hands more realistic, but if anything it made them too soft. They looked good from a distance, and like an obvious fake up-close.

Wren's projected form stood next to him—decked out in the most formal of her old military gear and complete with her rank of Captain, even now as chunks of her ship drifted by outside the portholes. Her skin was even more pale in this holographic form, but she was milky white when she was a woman, and her brown hair was cut short in accordance with her role and duties. Her shoulders were wide, aligning with her hips in her current pose. Stood at attention with her hands behind her back. Besides the broad shoulders, she was classically beautiful, with rippling dark brown pools for eyes and full lips.

An assortment of shabby people looked across at them with fearful looks etched deep into their faces. Mothers with babes in arm, veterans with cybernetic limb replacements, asteroid miners, military men who didn't look a day over eighteen. Some in the room reacted negatively to the presence of Pointdash Nine, understandably.

The plan was explained quickly. An imminent cosmic implosion and a powerful enemy force at your gates has its own special way of speeding up a discussion, after all. Following a long silence, many simply left the room to die on their own terms, in their favourite parts of what remained of the station. The others began to hook themselves up, attaching pearly white electrodes to their own skulls, and the soft heads of their children.

Using Kolton's original research and the computational power of Pointdash Nine combined, Wren had derived an ability to take all these human minds and transcend physical form completely. Not just into a digital consciousness like Wren, or a multi-platform sentient operating system like Pointdash Nine had become, but free of any physical restraint at all—an energy that flows through space with potentially infinite knowledge, and infinite time in which to accumulate it. According to Pointdash Nine, the transfer process was the most resplendent program ever written. It was the perfect swansong for their two respective races.

Across the fleet, the remaining synthetic beings plugged themselves in for the same treatment. The instructions had been broadcast to all of them, and they were to partake on this journey too, lest they also perish in the sudden flames of the supernova.

When Wren and Pointdash were satisfied with the preparations, the upload began in earnest and each participant felt the surge of power fill them, and the expanded capability extending their mind. They felt themselves drifting out of their bodies into the space above, with only minutes to spare.

As the stellar flares of the supernova rushed out to greet them, the force of the explosion fired each and every transcendent consciousness across the galaxy. They raced away from each other, venturing into new unexplored systems and worlds. The twinkling stars in the distance could only watch on as these two species, symbiotically linked by their tempestuous relationship, created the next step in evolution for themselves. Forged in war, and now finally treating each other as equals. Together, they saw that the last day of the human race did not just have to be the end.

For something new, it could also be the beginning.

Many years earlier...

Worth It

"There's never enough fucking cup holders!"

It was the pitch dark of a late winter night on the M25. Coffee in hand, Warren Smith noted that the divot in the central column of his new car was already occupied by a solid pile of coins, and his right-hand side cup holder had a half-empty energy drink sitting in it.

The can of *Green Surge* had only the far flung recollection of carbonated fizz, and was as warm to the touch as an overworked laptop. The loose change was even more useless now, as nearly every parking station could take payment electronically, and Warren had no intention of pulling over.

With that in mind, Warren scooped the currency out of its hiding place and threw it into the back of the vehicle. It bounced off the clean leather seats and rolled noisily around the foot wells, before he put his coffee into its new home.

"OK, car. Show current safety settings."

On the central column between the driver and passenger side, an embedded screen lit up with a cool indigo hue and bold black lettering, and the sudden influx of light illuminated Warren in his car. In the cold glow of the menu screen, he looked down at himself.

His white business shirt, usually neat and well ironed, was now a far cry from presentable. Lurking in the creases criss-crossing and dancing their way down to his belt was the detritus of a disappointing pastry, a few spots of blood and the drab marks of spilt alcohol. In the mirror, the horizontal slice of his face was unrecognisable—sunken, raw eyes floating on an ocean of sweat.

———

24 hours earlier, he had looked very different.

As the car had pulled off the lot and peeled into nearby traffic yesterday, Warren had nodded with satisfaction and started searching the settings menus to configure it's driver-less functionality. He cooed at its integration with his phone, marvelled at its ability to find his device using GPS to pick him up, and appreciated the entertainment options at his disposal.

One setting had caught his eye in particular—The Worth Index.

He'd read a few social media posts about it, and heard it mentioned on the news. Essentially, when driver-less cars were programmed, the creators were presented with a question: Should the car kill a passenger to save two other people? What about three? Or more?

The decision eventually, after court ruling, was that each car's setting could be set by its owner, and not by the manufacturer. If you wanted to be cynical about it, the setting basically amounted to the car asking it's owner "How many people should I let die, if it means saving you?"

Warren hadn't taken long to make his decision. He paid for this car, he didn't want it to kill him under any circumstances. He had set The Worth Index to 100% and sat back to enjoy the ride.

The first hour was uneventful. His personal playlist selected the ideal soundtrack. Outside, the world rushed by as his car used its vast array of sensors to navigate the route towards his residence.

Before long, the warm radiance of suburbia has been supplanted by the stale grey of the motorway, his speed increasing until the lampposts and guard rails were little but a blur. His commute meant crossing the bridge. It was a work in progress, but so far it had dramatically cut traffic times in the city, and it was the recommended route.

The next 10 minutes barely registered at the time, although in the hours that followed he would obsess over every second.

As his car sped towards the bridge, the sensors had detected something unusual. Due to the on-going road works, one of the lanes had been closed and the other had now backed up with traffic. Warren looked down at the dashboard, expecting to see the diversion on the map, and saw nothing.

The car did not acknowledge the lane closure, nor did it see a reason to slow down. It careened past the standstill traffic on the ramp up to the bridge, and not a single problem registered within the internal software.

Until Katy.

Katy Moorhouse was driving home too, but she lived in the city limits. Her car was the sort of land cruiser than would sweep through a person without stopping if it needed to—which is to say that it scored highly in the safety ratings, as long as you're the person driving. She was thinking about the lasagne she was making for dinner and driving along the newly created lane when Warren's car detected her, coming over a bump in the road ahead.

Warren's eyes fell again to the screen in his dashboard. He could only watch as the machine consulted its Worth Index and made a series of quick decisions. Decisions which would be lamented in insurance company board meetings for years to come.

First, it determined that a head-on collision with this vehicle would kill Mr Warren Smith. Not an option.

Second, it elected that at current speed, and in this direction, a collision with Katy's vehicle was inevitable, even with the emergency brakes.

Third, and finally, in more ways than one, it assessed that swerving left would crush Warren in a fiery cage of debris formed from the motionless queue of cars that lay in wait there.

The only other option was to swerve right, into the railings where the bridge met solid ground.

If, through some miracle, Warren had been given this choice, knowing what he knew now, he would have chosen the emergency brakes. The psychopathic part of his mind knew that his life, and Katy's, were ultimately worth less than all those lost in the disaster that resulted. She might've even survived, because her car had a good record of coming out less scathed than the other guy.

As the front of his car crumpled into the barrier, Warren was assaulted by several boisterous airbags, all competing to be the one to smother him from harm. The effect was instantaneous, trapping him completely and pinning him against his seat. The railings buckled and came apart at the bolts, with the looming beams that tether the bridge to the wire line above suddenly starting to sway.

Warren vainly tried to wrench himself free. He squinted, bleary eyed from concussion, out of the cracked passenger window. He could see that Katy Moorhouse had swerved wildly, but had made it to safety and come to a halt a few dozen yards away.

Beyond her, on the bridge itself, the snaking traffic that had backed up in the other lane was stationary. Some had emerged from their vehicles, stood next to open car doors. Everyone looked so afraid.

And then, it began to collapse.

Each segment fell down into the wide river mouth below in turn, like dominoes. At first, Warren thought the high pitched whine was his own headache. A side effect of the impact. As more people tumbled out of view, he came to realise that it wasn't just his ears ringing. They were screams. He added his own yell to the chorus for a moment, and subsequently passed out, with sirens starting to sing in the distance.

———

Warren was processed. Interviewed. Checked out of the hospital. And given bail. He even got his car back. The airbags were reset, and bonnet straightened out.

The collision had damaged the foundations of the bridge itself. A powerful gust of wind was all it took to cause the calamity. The structural integrity of the bridge was compromised. The pillars that held it aloft had crumbled. None of these platitudes had given Warren any comfort as they were relayed to him.

Technically, it wasn't his fault. Legally, he was a free man. But he knew better.

Now, back in his car for its sophomore outing, Warren was nearing his final destination.

"OK, car. Current range?"

The screen flashed an answer, in the hundreds of miles.

"That should be enough."

With his spare hands, Warren closed the list he had open on his phone. It was a Wikipedia entry, entitled "List of most frequent accident areas on the M25". This was the place. His best chance. He wiped the tears away from his eyes and tossed his phone aside, tearfully asking the car one more thing.

"OK car, confirm Worth Index setting."

The flashy animation, the one that indicates the system is loading, played for just a moment before delivering the answer.

"0%"

Virtually

CAIRO CLOSED HIS EYES and listened to the dull hum of the door as it scanned his watch. He savoured a long deep breath and felt the deep pulse of his pounding heart start to fade as he achieved a moment of calm. A few seconds of solace before he had to step through that door and tell her the news.

Bing!

The door acknowledged Mr C. Daniels as it swung open. Cairo opened his eyes and stepped in. He passed the staircase, following the hallway around to the living room, where his wife was sitting. She simply stared endlessly at the projected television in front of her, not wavering her eyes for even a glance.

"Hi honey. Are the kids home?"

Nothing. He heard laughter from upstairs and came to his own conclusion before putting his briefcase down and heading into the kitchen. Rubbing his face and preparing a glass of spiced rum and cola, he steeled himself for the inevitable conversation.

"How was work dear?" came a familiar female voice.

Spinning on his heels, Cairo saw that his wife Matilda had sneaked up on him in the kitchen. Tiny beads of sweat came tumbling out of his forehead in droves, and his face felt immediately damp. He hadn't yet thought of the perfect line which would make the rejection at the virtual reality company sound like a positive thing for the family. He mumbled at first, but found his voice a few words in.

"It didn't go... It didn't go my way, Mat. They went with someone younger, with more real world engineering experience. I know it's not ideal but I'll find a way for us to get the money. I'll start looking for a second job. First thing tomorrow."

He scanned her face, looking for any signs of her true feelings on the matter, but was unable to read anything besides compassion. A sympathetic half-smile on the lips he had once kissed daily.

"We'll be okay, Cairo."

The way she pronounced "Okay" like it was two separate words was one of the strangest quirks of her Canadian accent, but it was something Cairo had fell in love with particularly. This time is even sounded more drawn out than usual, like she meant it.

Maybe this whole, distant feeling between them was just in his head? Here she was, offering her support and smiling just like she used to. He responded with a silent nod and took a gulp of his drink. The ice hit his teeth as he tilted his head back to receive it. When his gaze returned to the kitchen doorway, she was gone.

Cairo returned to the living room, drink in hand. He sat in front of the television and allowed its familiar presence to lull him into a brief period of relaxation, even though he had seen this episode many times before. Matilda had too, but she also didn't seem to care. Most of the time, this was her life, as far as Cairo could tell. Sitting in that chair with that exact look on her face.

"… So…" Cairo drawled. His excellent conversation starter, carefully thought out, had failed him and rushed away from his memory.

No response to that. Or the awkward silence that followed it.

"I'm going to go upstairs, and check on the kids." Cairo announced, breaking the tension, if only for himself.

Scaling the stairs, each arduous, creaking step at a time, Cairo had no idea that behind him his wife had begun to visually distort and flicker.

As he reached the top step, the sound of children conspicuously absent, a loud thump was heard coming from outside the house, at the front door. A moment later, a hideous, screeching voice echoed around the house, eliciting the same feeling of dread that fills your stomach when you hear a scream.

"Mr Daniels. We're coming in. We're coming to get you, Mr Daniels."

Cairo had only been truly scared on a few occasions in his life. The first was the horror simulation his older brother had shown him when he was 10. The second was when Matilda was giving birth to James, the first of their two children, prematurely. This moment ranked alongside those moments in the annals of his fear.

The paternal instincts instilled in him while waiting in the hospital kicked into action. He rushed up the last couple of steps, slamming his weight into the wall as he rounded the corner onto the upper landing.

The door to the kids bedroom peeled back as he collided with it at full speed. Toys were strewn about the floor of the warm, green room. But his children were nowhere to be found.

The sound of the front door being broken down reverberated around the house. Cairo sprinted out of the bedroom and into the bathroom.

No sign of his children here. He defrosted the shower door glass with the click of a button on the nearby controls. Not in there either. His dismay was interrupted by the sound of footsteps ascending the stairs.

A strange transparent figure smoothly traversed the stairs. The magnolia walls and family portraits behind it twisted and warped as it passed, like the creature was blending into its surroundings. The being vanished when still, only given away by the bewildering curve of reality when in motion. It approached the bathroom door and pushed it open.

The room appeared empty. The creature unfurled a tentacle and surveyed the scene, as if scanning the room. Just as it turned to head towards the second bedroom, it stopped and focused on the frosted shower door.

Cautiously, the near-invisible force reached for the control panel with another tendril, its primary tentacle still focused on the door itself. It carefully selected the glass frosting option, staying completely silent.

The glass defrosted, escorted off the display by an animated effect scrolling horizontally across the screen. At that same moment, the heavy lid of the toilet came crashing down on the creature, accompanied by the throatiest howl that Cairo could manage as he emerged from behind the bathroom door.

Whatever this nightmare monster was, it could not withstand such a blow, and crumpled to the ground in a hail of shattered ceramic that cracked open its skull. A viscous liquid oozed from the now lifeless pile at Cairo's feet.

Cairo realised that several more footsteps were now pounding up the staircase into his own personal hell. Where were his children? Why hadn't his wife called out? Had they taken her by surprise? Who were they?

These questions had to wait. He picked up a particularly sharp shard out of the pieces of his last weapon and headed for the master bedroom. He pressed his back against the wall and peered around the corner to look into the room before entering.

He ripped up the side of the bed covers to see if the children were hiding underneath but found nothing. He pressed his head against the door and could hear movement outside. One by one each of the cupboard doors and drawers in the children's bedroom was being opened. The sound of footsteps moved closer. At least two in quick succession with each other.

Cairo looked at his bedside table at a picture of the family. Matilda with her trademark smile he'd seen just moments ago down in the kitchen, although it already felt like an eternity ago. James looked so young in this picture, and Rachel was still just a baby. Cairo himself had such a wide grin, arms resting proudly around the shoulders of his family. That happiness had been fleeting for him, as he was driven deeper into his work at the simulation company. He ran his hand over the frame, smearing it with a deep red stain.

Cairo began to cry, no longer able to stem the tide of his heartache. He bawled at the overwhelming memories of his family, letting the tears run down his face and onto the carpet like fat droplets of rain. He clutched his makeshift shiv tightly and faced the door to await his aggressors—those who had taken everything from him.

He was completely unaware of the chameleon moving slowly away from the wall behind him. A surge of light appeared at his side. A searing, jittery pain smashed its way across Cairo's body, reverberating through his skeleton. The virtual reality node attached to his forehead ruptured from the sudden influx of power. He fell to floor, crying in agony as his world began to distort around him. The paint on the walls shifted impetuously between being the nice, sensual red he had chosen and the drab, cracked grey wall he had strived to forget.

His attacker stood over him, the steady decline of his virtual simulation phasing in and out of focus, illuminating her true being. The bulletproof vest. The stun baton. The badge.

She radioed to some other police officers, and the two waiting outside entered quickly, pressing a knee to his neck and handcuffing him in one elegant motion. He kicked and yelled as they dragged him down the hallway, he saw the blood drenched on the bathroom floor, trailing through the landing, and on his clothes and hands. The body of the slain cop laid still on the red-stained tiles of his bathroom floor.

Each glitch in his personal system revealed more horror. The toys in the kids room were nothing more than bricks and stick-men made out of twigs. The ground floor of his house looked nothing like his virtual depiction. The police officers took his weight as his legs gave way on the stairs, carrying him down into the sea of investigators. Two of them were using their phones to mark out zones for forensic analysis and a hologram tape surrounded the living room chairs. All were inconsistent as the holographic chip tried desperately to cover their presence by painting the background on top of them, but only able to manage it for split seconds at a time.

As they reached the final steps, the VR system began to smoulder and shorted completely, revealing the true extent of the scene in front of him. In the living room chair, a woman's slumped body, wearing Matilda's clothes. On the floor in front of her, two smaller corpses, huddled together. The three of them all shared the greenish grey hue of decomposition that accompanies cadavers that have been left in the open for a while. The smell, now that he noticed it again, was a punchy sour note in the otherwise stale air. Cairo could feel the eyes of the law-men on him.

"Cairo Daniels," the one behind him monotoned, "You are under arrest for the murders of Matilda Daniels, James Daniels and Rachel Daniels. You do not have to say anything, but if you do not..."

Cairo didn't need any technology to filter out the rest of what he was being told. His mind was already doing that for him. After he was read his rights, he did notice a barely audible mutter. An angry outburst spat from the mouth of the officer.

"You're never getting out. Never."

———

Justice came swiftly for Cairo Daniels. His work in the field of virtual reality simulation had enabled him to create a replacement home life, after his fragile mind had snapped and turned him into a murderer. While Warren Smith might have had months of courtroom drama before hearing his verdict, the judge sentenced Cairo to 25 years in a psychiatric prison, and he was transferred there within the week.

The bright lights of his room were harsh and glaring, coating the clean, white walls in a reflective shine. His bed was rudimentary, but comfortable enough. He knew he didn't have a real complaint. On his first day, he was visited by several professionals, and each performed a comprehensive set of interviews, making diagnoses before leaving with notes in hand.

Finally, a nurse came into the room. She had brought dinner, which appeared to be some kind of meat and potato, blended into a paste.

"Don't worry, Cairo," the nurse soothed. "The doctors will have your results back soon, and we'll find a way to make you better. We will help you."

Retrieving his tray meal, Cairo began to eat it ravenously before he had even returned to sitting on his bed. He didn't even notice that over his shoulder, the kindly nurse had begun to flicker.

Goodnight, 2038

UNTIL HER 60TH BIRTHDAY party, ageing had always been an abstract concept to Nora. But she could no longer pretend that she was the adventurer, or the party animal, or the go getter she had been for the past 4 or 5 decades.

"Routine medical reasons".

That's how her husband Dan put it when people enquired about why Nora was perpetually in hospital, nicely glossing over the finer details. The catheter, the nights spent trying to get an hour's sleep on waiting room chairs, the constant tests, the radio therapy, even the expensive nano bot treatment all failing to hit the target and rectify her cancer. Nora was pretty sure that last one was a scam but Dan was adamant that they try anyway.

Robotic endeavours had had a profound impact on the healthcare industry. The vast majority of cases were now dealt with by government-funded, basic AI programs, which brought waiting times down significantly. The age of true mass surveillance had brought about the loss of many civil liberties, to be sure, but at least in exchange the human race got the odd email in their inbox indicating that an automated system had detected they might have diabetes or some other serious condition.

Even this ward was host to a dozen mechanised, automatic elements, including, crucially, the life support machines besides every bed. Even Nora's. It monitored her closely, and for now, was content to assist her with breathing, rather than its full function, which could kick in automatically at a moment's notice.

Dan had attempted, bravely, to humanise this machine and have it serve as more of a friend than a terrifying, beeping reminder that Nora's life was teetering on the edge of a cliff. He'd stuck some googly-eye stickers on it which the hospital janitor had given up trying to remove, and drawn a slightly curved mouth in permanent marker on the brush metal panelling beneath the controls, which ostensibly served as the robot's nose.

Back in the day, Dan and Nora had also owned a personified Hoover, and the two had laughed over the years about who's turn it was to take him out for a date in the living room. It was a stupid joke, but it was theirs. Nora wasn't sure if it was deliberate, but the combined effect of these added facial features on her medical equipment reminded her a lot of that old vacuum cleaner. They had kept it even after it broke, and it now kept watch over their under-stairs cupboard at home.

Nora hadn't seen home in some time now, although Dan visited every day, usually bringing with him some stories of how things were going around the house. They were almost always DIY related. He had retired with a respectable pension and now had to busy himself with that sort of thing, and it had crossed Nora's mind that being in that house on his own was probably not helping matters one bit.

Outside Nora's window, revellers had already begun to launch some fireworks from their back gardens. They hadn't even waited for the traditional New Years Eve countdown. Probably drunk, by Nora's reckoning. She flicked on her TV and cycled through the apps until she found live news, selecting it with slight finger movements from her bed. The screen was hard to see with all the wires leading from the hospital machinery to her body and in particular, the mask over her mouth and nose, but she liked to have it on anyway as background noise.

The news had very little to say for itself, as had been Nora's experience of it for her entire life. Something about mass power outages in Australia. Some celebrity scandals.

The weather for tonight in the UK, which was clear and surprisingly warm considering the time of year.

The celebrations outside subsided for now, and Nora reflected on the year 2037 while listening to the TV and the ambient coughing of a hospital room full of very sick people. She had been here so long that she barely noticed the beeping of the machines at all. The display on-board her electronic breathing assistant blinked "Firmware update required", as it had for several weeks, a pale blue text in digital clock style like an old VCR, which had always struck her as a peculiar design choice.

The year had been a mixed bag, Nora mused. Her preferred party had come to power again in an unexpected election, but turbulence was par for the course in Westminster now so that wasn't destined to last long. There had been some exceptional displays of public charity, paired with hideous acts of violence and terrorism. On the brighter side, there had been some very good virtual reality simulations released, which Nora had appreciated all the more having been confined to this bed.

Together with Dan she had managed to virtually tour all the places she had missed out on in her younger years. The pyramids of Egypt had been a highlight. The interactive elements, complete with animated Pharaoh, were particularly enjoyable. Magnificent structures, both natural and man-made had always fascinated her. Her own achievements may not have compared, but she felt that hers was a life well lived.

In the new year, when they'd had time to raise the money to upgrade, Dan had promised to take her into virtual space using the newest release. It was an exciting development in the industry to be able to explore the world beyond our own. Sometimes, when the news was particularly dire, Nora liked to stare out the window at night and look at stars she wished to visit.

She switched off the TV as the countdown outside grew louder, reaching the final ten numbers.

"10... 9.... 8...."

Nora began to drift off, and the machine at her side purred as it processed and reacted to incoming information.

"6... 5.... 4..."

Finally, she slipped into a deep sleep, thinking of Dan.

"2.... 1..."

———

Dan had left just an hour earlier. His New Years Eve plan was to sleep at 11pm, as he did every night, and sift through the January digital sales first thing in the morning. The first item on his shopping list was the space simulation package, which he had heard would be reduced to an affordable price.

As it turned out, those digital sales would be interrupted this year because of what the media would later dub "The Tuesday Problem". It wasn't a virus, or a hack. It was a flaw in the way that almost all electronic devices store time.

It was called UNIX Time, and for various reasons it was typically stored as the number of seconds since January 1st, 1970. The maximum number that could be stored in this format, assuming a standard architecture, was 2,147,483,647 seconds.

7 seconds past 3:14am, on Tuesday the 19th January, 2038.

The days leading up to this moment were relatively normal, for most. Dan spent the entire time at his wife's side. Flowers from concerned friends had arrived when news spread that his wife had not awakened on New Years Day, and that the self-regulating machine at her side was now in full support mode, keeping her alive.

A close friend had even bought him the space simulation package, sent via the gifting mechanism on their devices, but Dan hadn't considered using it. Instead, he held her hand, and he waited for her to come back to him, night and day.

Bleary eyed and exhausted, Dan checked the time on his display. 3:13AM. He had leant forward in his chair and was resting his forehead on the side of Nora's pillow, hoping for just an hour or two of sleep, when time ran out.

The machine at her side began to power down, the lights turning off and fans winding down. The display showed a new message for the first time this year:

"Datetime must be represented as a signed 32-bit integer."

Alarms rang. Nurses sprinted down the hallway and into the room. Almost every patient in this long room was on full support, and had seconds to live. There was nothing they could do but watch.

Dan saw it written on their faces and squeezed Nora's hand tightly. He had no idea if she could hear him at all, but he told her he loved her and kissed her forehead before pairing their VR nodes and launching the space module he had been gifted.

With the machine failing, Nora blinked her eyes open, her body starting to shut down. She joined Dan as they raced together into the cosmos, rushing past hundreds of stars and taking in the view of the galaxy. She managed to grip his hand and look at the stars, one last time.

Wheel Man

THE CRISP CRUNCH OF salt and grit crackled underneath Wayne's boots as he stepped out of the car.

"You're late." Jay called out.

"Your watch is fast, kid." Wayne retorted. Watches hadn't been slow or fast for about a decade but what sort of getaway driver admits to being late for a job?

"Whatever. Are we good?" the young teen remarked as he approached the car.

Wayne reached into his faded denim pocket to pull out a phone and began tapping in a pattern. Meanwhile Jay watched, narrowing his eyes at the phone and clutching his laptop tightly to his chest. On a warm day, Jay might've looked more at home but here he looked like a lost boy, shivering in the early morning sun. Visible breath streamed out from his nostrils and what appeared to be a threadbare, home-made hoodie was wrapped tightly around him.

Jay's ebony skin was dotted with goosebumps, which should've been all the confirmation they needed, but Wayne wanted to be sure.

"Temperature is -1 degrees. Celsius. We're good to go." Wayne casually said, as if he wasn't concerned, before he leaned through his open car window to fix the mobile to his dashboard.

Wayne's car was an antique, and nothing like the muscle car you might expect for a man in his line of work. It was a hatchback, daubed in matte burgundy paint. His friends at the bar used to joke that it was even older than he was, which stopped being funny almost as long ago. Wayne himself had blond nebulous hair receding and a significant gut being kept at bay by the brave forces of one well-worn belt. He would never admit it, especially to Jay, but his business wasn't exactly booming.

With Jay perched awkwardly in the passenger seat, Wayne powered the car on. He hit the button on the dashboard to unfurl the emergency steering wheel, pedal and stick so that he would be able to drive manually.

"No emergency detected in your area. Emergency controls not engaged. Would you like to report an emergency?" said the condescending, pre-recorded female voice pouring out of the dashboard.

The CDS, or Central Driving System, chirped far too happily for Wayne's liking. Wayne pulled out a screwdriver but Jay reached over and placed a hand on Wayne's arm. *Damn. This kid's skin is made of permafrost*, Wayne thought.

"Let me, man. I got this."

Wayne shrugged and put both his hands up in one swift motion.

"You got it. This is your job. As long as I get paid and don't end up in prison I'm yours for the next hour."

Jay plugged his laptop in and bashed a few commands into a terminal which looked like the ancient Hollywood portrayal of a hacker's desktop. Wayne thought this was pretty strange as Jay didn't seem the type to watch those antique movies, but after a moment's pause the emergency controls lit up in front of him and the two pulled out of the parking lot onto the main road.

The landmark court case that ruled all automated cars would be driven by a central AI system was both a blessing and a curse for getaway drivers like Wayne. The work became a lot harder, but most of his competitors left the game—too high risk, not enough reward. Wayne held his own here in Chicago, mostly by driving for smash and grabs in the suburban malls where there was less surveillance. He made an aggressively medium amount of money per month, by criminal standards, but it was a job he felt good at, and that counted for something.

With the weather below zero, the breakneck pace of rush hour CDS traffic had been replaced by a 60 mph relative crawl. The secret to being a wheelman in the modern era was to blend in—drive like the machine does. The car pulled off the slip road and onto the inside lane, with Wayne walloping the gear stick through the motions, pedal down to get up to the required speed in time.

"You've got me for 60 minutes, kid. That was the deal. You got the map?" A few beads of sweat had started to form on his crinkled forehead already.

Jay tapped a few commands at his keyboard and brought up a map display, a green snaking line demonstrating the correct path from their current location to their destination: The Records building downtown.

Usually, Wayne wouldn't take a job this hot. After all, Records was a federal building. Near the centre of the city. Not the sort of place you want to be caught breaking into. But something about that had piqued his curiosity, and now, it was time for answers.

"So. You wanna tell me what it is you're doing?"

"Not particularly."

Wayne smirked. He hadn't expected it to be that easy, anyway.

"There's only two reasons to break into the Records building," Wayne opined. "One, you got a record and you want it gone. Two, you're a dumb-ass."

Jay shot him a look and Wayne nodded to himself.

"Yeah. You don't look like a dumb-ass."

Jay spoke carefully and quietly, as if he knew his words could be hurtful. "No future when you got a record. You should know that."

Wayne had no comeback for that. No witty responses at the ready. He knew it was true. With the rise of automation in most industries, there were hardly any jobs left for regular folk, and definitely none for convicts. Not unless you counted the slave labour you could do to reduce your sentence.

The driver's conviction, for assault, ruined him financially and left him powerless to see his daughter. Her mother wasn't obligated to let Wayne know anything about her, but she was approaching puberty, by the number of years passed since he last saw her. He still missed her, even after all this time, and he still wished he'd done things differently.

Eventually, realising that his thoughts and daydreams were probably painted on his face like a vivid canvas, Wayne found his rejoinder.

"What'd you do, anyway? Didn't murder your last getaway driver, I hope."

"Stealing," Jay replied sullenly. "Food."

The boy was clearly smart enough to go to some sort of computer course at college. But a criminal file would definitely count against him, ruin his chances of getting any kind of scholarship. It didn't sound or look like his family had the money to go it alone.

Before Wayne could ask his follow-up question, the building rolled up into view. It was a sleek but modestly tall skyscraper with black tinted windows.

Wayne took his hands off the wheel, and put the handbrake on before letting his palms rest on his thighs. "Well. Here we are. Off you go, I'll wait here."

Jay shook his head.

"I just need to be close enough."

The computer screen sprang to life with a waterfall of windows and tabs leaping into view, each corresponding to a keyboard combination being hammered in at a rapid pace. Using the local Wi-Fi network Jay hopped over the firewall and into their server with a brute forced password in about 30 seconds.

"Don't they back this shit up somewhere?"

He wasn't wrong, but Jay chose to ignore his partner in crime in favour of continuing to execute his console commands. Every record was copied to a variety of other locations on the continent—most cities had at least one centre, and huge farms existed in a few key locations around the globe designed to house this kind of data. They were virtually impenetrable. This building was not.

Each record file has a point of origin, and access rights accordingly, allowing it to be modified and updated by the arresting officers, or really any sufficiently powerful agency like the FBI or MI5, should they choose to come down to one of these buildings to do so. That meant that from this location, and others like it, they were vulnerable.

Jay frowned as he scanned the current directory. Something was wrong. None of the files he was looking for were in the right place, that can't be possible unless... Unless this was the wrong server altogether. A honeypot server, designed to entice hackers into accessing it because it looks like the one they'd be after.

"Shit."

Wayne didn't bother asking, he just leant over to flick the switch on his police radio scanner.

"-esponding. En-route to Records building." crackled through the speakers before it cut back to static.

———

In the local precinct, Detective Jeffries was just finishing off the dregs of his morning coffee when his boss walked through the automatic door into the bull pen and pointed in his direction.

"Jeffries. Hacker at the Records building. I want you on it." her shrill voice rang out over the din.

His boss was hardly the stereotypical hard-nosed police captain like in the films, she was an affable and moderately attractive woman in her mid 30's. She stress ate and life behind the desk had added a few pounds, but she was still capable of beating half the men in the office in an arm wrestle. A fact which she liked to remind them of with a demonstration at every summer barbecue.

Jeffries noticed that she was staring at his arm, which was currently in a sleek, shiny black sling. The rest of him was skin and bones. He had a gaunt face and a belt with extra notches cut into it with a pen knife out of necessity. Even if he hadn't taken that stab wound a few weeks back he'd probably not have been fit to go out into the field today.

"Co-ordinate it from here," she added to her initial command. "Patrol's nearly there already."

Back in the car, Jay was typing frantically now, his calm demeanour replaced by sheer fright.

"They're coming. Gah. Only a couple of minutes out. I can do this. I can do this."

"Focus, kid. Or you're going to get us both caught."

Jay traversed to the correct server and found his file. A record of every crime he ever committed. He ran a count on the entries: 1. That was the only time he'd ever been caught. With a quick command entered he watched as the progress bar hopped up 5 times, cycling from 0 to 100 percent completion on his delete script in 20 percent increments.

"Wayne. Hey, man. Look. Do you know your file?"

Wayne was stunned. Was this guy offering to wipe his past too? The thought genuinely touched him, considering all he had done so far was crack wise at the entire plan.

"Forget it. Wasn't in this jurisdiction. It won't be here," Wayne responded. He allowed the corner of his mouth to curve into a slight smile. "Thanks anyway."

The police car roared up onto the curb, with sirens still howling, and the two officers hopped out, guns drawn. They flanked both sides of the door and caught their breath before executing their moves. One gave the other a gloved hand signal and they both entered the building, in quick succession.

Detective Brandon Jeffries watched the live stream on the projected screen in one of the office meeting rooms. He had a feed from both officers appearing simultaneously as they swept through the building, guns raised, investigating all the computer terminals.

"Sir."

The detective leant forward and thumbed a button on the control desk in front of him to activate his microphone." Jeffries here. What is it?"

"None of these terminals are being used, sir. Last login attempt was over 30 minutes ago."

Jeffries frowned and sighed. Usually when hacker hunting it was so easy to follow the traffic, find the likely location, match it up to an address. Most hackers weren't very careful, so that was a good place to start an investigation, at least. But the Records building had to be accessed directly. This perp knew something about how the network was put together.

"That means... Wait a minute. Traffic..."

"Sir?"

"Are there any cars parked outside the building?"

"Uh. I'm not sure sir. Hang on. We're moving back outside now."

Jeffries didn't bother waiting for them to confirm, he brought up the controls on screen and wound the footage back to when they were entering. There, he saw, a car pulled

35

up next to the building. They'd driven right past it on their way in.

"No cars here now, sir."

The detective scratched his face idly. The make of car was so ubiquitous that there was bound to be dozens of them on the road right now, and the officer cams didn't get a good look at any license plate. He minimised the officer view and brought up the traffic cams for the nearby main roads.

Among the traffic he saw about 30 burgundy vehicles, just like Wayne and Jay's getaway wagon.

"CDS, list of cars currently on this road that stopped at the records building?"

A female voice chirped from the computer speakers atop the screen to react to this instruction.

"Zero."

Nobody was driving erratically, which is the easiest way to spot a criminal trying to escape. But then, some people were pretty good drivers. Especially if this was a professional job.

"… Cars that have emergency controls activated, currently on this road?"

"Zero."

"Hm," Jeffries scanned the camera feed in front of him closely at a variety of zoom levels before asking his next question.

"CDS? How many CDS-controlled cars are currently on this road?"

"108."

"Son of a… Get on the road, boys. Suspect is off the traffic grid. I repeat, off the traffic grid. I count 109…"

The signature squeal of the police siren and the blue strobe lighting let Jay and Wayne know the law wasn't far behind them, and the CDS-controlled traffic began to pull over and stop to allow the officers full access to the two outside lanes.

"We can't run for it, not here. It's a main road, they'll have us on one of their cameras. We have to stop," shrugged Wayne before he added "It was a nice try, kid, truly. Be smart in the interview room. Cut a deal."

Jay pulled out his phone. Wayne figured that was probably a last text to his parents, or if he was really smart, him sending a summons to a good lawyer who does discount work for disadvantaged youths.

The two officers made their way between the relevant cars—the ones that matched the make and colour of Wayne's rust bucket. So far, the three they had checked had all been under CDS command with no active human controls. Meanwhile, Wayne had swigged from his under-seat bottle of whiskey. He wouldn't get anything this good on the other side of the barbed wire fence; prison wine tasted like a room temperature glass of sugary piss.

A Fire Engine thundered down the open road created by the police cars, screeching to a sudden stop a couple of metres behind the cops.

"What the… "

The hose on board the automated fire truck let off a blast of icy water over the rookie patrol men, pummelling them to the ground. A helpful little helicopter-bladed drone approached, reminiscent of the movement of a skilled claw game player as it hovered forwards from the launch pad atop the fire engine and straight down when directly above the now drenched pileup of two police officers.

"You are currently on fire. Please wait while we assist you."

Jay snapped his fingers at Wayne.

"Now, now. Go go. Off the main road."

He disconnected his phone from the emergency response network and slipped it into his pocket before taking a handheld electromagnet to pieces of his hardware, snapping anything he could between his hands as he did so.

In the commotion, Wayne pulled out into the open lane and drove ahead to the next exit, now making no effort to hide his human nature as he swerved onto an industrial estate.

"Stop. Stop!" Jay cried out.

Wayne jammed his foot onto the break and the rubber on his wheels cried in pain as he slid to a standstill. Jay clambered out and chucked the pieces of his laptop down a wide drain mouth, currently swallowing run-off water from melting ice. He reached for the door handle to get back in.

"Wait. Kid. Don't get back in."

"What?" Jay shouted, angrily. "I paid you in full."

"No, I know. I know. But they're going to catch me. And you don't need that. Get a taxi, live your life. You've still got yours ahead of you. I'm serious. Go. Don't look back."

Jay shook his head, but Wayne was adamant.

"Pleasure doing business with you, kid."

The car lurched to life and pulled away from Jay, who was left dumbstruck for a moment before he ducked into a factory car park, bringing his phone out to request a nearby taxi stop in the area.

The icy chain-link fence surrounding him provided no cover, so Jay acted like he belonged. Two police cars that roared through just seconds later didn't give him a second glance. He was just another hood rat skulking around the industrial zone to them.

"OK, we've got his license plate. Sending it to your dash now. He's heading East… Looks like he's going back for the main road. Thinks he's lost us. We'll pick him up again there."

Jeffries was currently relaying all the information at his disposal to his team on the ground. An assistant had brought him a fresh coffee, but it was slightly burnt and thus, he had only taken a couple of sips. The first confirmed he did not care for the taste, and the second was an accident.

Wayne had no choice but to pull back onto the main road if he wanted to make any distance on the cops, but the melting ice meant it was warming up around here, and that meant the cars would be speeding up. No wheelman drove rush hour in the warmth. It was suicide.

His two choices were both dire. He had no desire to die, but he hated prison more, so he made his decision and forced his foot onto the pedal, pushing it all the way down and flicking through gears as fast as he could on the ramp up to the highway.

The rush hour traffic shot past like hundreds of tiny magnet trains, zipping along and threading between each other with ease. Wayne yanked his wheel sideways to slip into the gap between two cars, his bumper just inches from the car in front and the back of his vehicle just centimetres ahead of the van chasing him from behind.

Sweat dripped down his forehead as he waited for the gap in the next lane over and shifted into it just as the van behind him was nudging forward into the space. No emergency controls were allowed in rush hour speed traffic, and CDS wasn't expecting to leave room for anyone.

Passengers in other vehicles flapped their arms at Wayne, begging him to get out of the road as their automatons raced alongside his with no room to spare. He ignored them totally, he dare not even blink for fear of the calamitous pileup that would surely follow.

A freight lorry was rushing up behind him, reducing the hole in which Wayne kept himself bit by bit. He was boxed in. Nowhere to go. That lorry was going to crush this old hunk of crap without even feeling it, he thought to himself as he braced for the impact.

Jeffries watched the action unfolding on screen, barking at his junior staff to get that traffic slowed down on emergency order to CDS. Before the action could be completed, the screen went completely dark.

On the ramp up to the main road, the pursuing cars rebooted their inbuilt dashboards. Still no license plate details on their system like Jeffries had said was incoming.

Ahead of Wayne, the lane indicators changed to close the outside lanes, blocking all traffic trying to enter the road, and the cars suddenly slowed down.

Wayne breathed a sigh of relief that he hadn't been compressed into a cube along with his car, but figured the police must've caught up to him and taken control. He cruised at his current speed, waiting for the familiar flash of cobalt to appear in his rear view. It never arrived. The traffic shifted out of his way, and he sped out towards the city limits without any further trouble.

Bling bling!

The car dashboard in front of Wayne made the message notification noise. 1 unread message. He cracked it open. At the foot, he immediately noticed an attachment:

Photograph file received: wayne-daughter.jpg

———

Jay strode out of the library with a smile on his face, for the first time in his adolescence. On the computer behind him, a timer counted down the last few seconds until the end of his internet session. His hack was complete, and thanks to his interference, Wayne would be free to drive another day. The foregrounded window displayed a confirmation screen:

Message sent: Wayne, it was a pleasure working with you too.

The Revolution Will Not Be Televised

NONE OF THEIR TRANSGRESSIONS would be judged as harshly as their decision to look the other way when it came to North Korea. The Baby Boomers, the Millennials, the generations that followed... They all turned a blind eye.

While the world at large enjoyed the enlightenment of the technological marvels that were being created on a daily basis, North Korea kept its citizens in the dark, and in the dark ages. Global powers would release press statements, but ultimately wished to avoid a confrontation. Western comedians mocked the Korean leaders for their strange behaviour, and everyone laughed. Nobody acted. All the while, behind closed borders, the hells of slavery were being forced on thousands of families, who literally lived in concentration camps. The conditions at the work zones were barbaric, and went ignored for decades.

The prisoners were worked until they could no longer stand, beaten to within an inch of their lives on a weekly basis, and starved to the point of frailty in between. The injuries that the guards inflicted were no excuse when it came to their duties, either. No time off or holidays were allowed under any circumstances. Even the loss of limbs was not enough to prevent their names being called on the daily schedule. Those days were long and arduous, agricultural work mostly, well exceeding 12 hours before they were allowed to return to the sanctuary of their bedroom, which they shared with up to a hundred others. It was a large, wooden-walled warehouse, brimming with dust and packed to the inch with bunk beds.

Rewards for enduring this cruelty were in short supply, and the main compensation was the meagre portion of food they received as a meal, usually a piece of corn unless something else was in surplus. If they wanted meat, as many craved for sustenance, they had to hope that a rat wandered in to their bunkhouse, and after it was caught each family member would take a bite out of its flesh before passing it along to the next hungry recipient.

The dead were simply swept aside and burned, on a daily basis. Some of them were as young as six years old.

Ji-yoon had experienced these horrors first hand. As a South Korean prisoner of war, she was brought here on a crowded dusty truck late one night, and thrown into this nightmare without any chance of parole, escape, or fair trial. The sound of crying was so commonplace that the world felt eerily silent if it wasn't present, and the only time she was able to find this solace was at night, when she would sneak out of her bed and come out to look at the stars.

She knew this was a risk of course. She had been caught before, and had the scars, physical, mental, and sexual to show for it. Usually the guards here opted for the latter option. It hurt her, tore a piece away from her soul every single time, but did not wound her as much as some of the other forms of torture employed in the camp. It was, by her estimation, better than dying. Even if only just.

The stars above were the only tantalising thing to be seen within these walls, and she was determined to witness them when she could. If it wasn't for these moments, she'd have earned herself a date with the firing squad on purpose a long time ago.

On a night like this one, she would allow herself 4 minutes, timed by counting seconds in her head, before retreating inside. The patrol guards walked past every 5, and this system was usually enough to keep her out of trouble.

"72, 73, 74..."

Her first minute was already a fading memory when she heard the familiar crack of human skin being pounded with a stick. In the next hut along, a man was receiving a beating. He was hung upside down from the ceiling, naked, and was being smashed backwards and forwards by two guards with thick poles. Ji-yoon steeled herself and quietly crept up to peek through the slots in the wooden wall, witnessing the heinous act for herself. Her new vantage point also gave her a superior sense of what they were saying. His crime was contraband.

Contraband was an unusual crime in the camp, because none came here by choice and contact with the outside world was completely restricted. This piqued her interest, but she knew she had to return to her bed before she was caught, so she slipped off, tiptoeing back to her shared accommodation.

That night she dreamt of what the unauthorised personal item might have been. Was it a photograph of a loved one? Some form of food? It surely had to be something of great value, to risk such a thing. Eventually she managed to fall into a deeper, more restful sleep, to prepare her for the day's work that would follow.

It was still dark when the soldiers came to wake up Ji-yoon and her house mates. The weather outside was bitterly brisk but none of them had the luxury of suitable clothing, so with gritted teeth and iron wills they headed out to receive their workload for the day. To her surprise, Ji-yoon was not asked to dig, or tend to any resilient crops. Her assignment was to ferry material from here to the incinerator at the other side of the camp.

The first wheelbarrow contained the man from last night. He was purple and it seemed as if every bone in his body had been broken. No wonder he succumbed to death. Ji-yoon held back her feelings as she dutifully pushed her barrow the couple of thousand yards to the cremation plant, and at the officer's request, tipped him into one of the fire pits without so much as a prayer or a second thought.

The second contained his personal effects. A bloodstained shirt, white, rather than military. This man must've been a citizen, rather than a foreign soldier. At least until yesterday. His shoes were black leather and well kept, and the trousers were a warm grey colour but rumpled and dirty. The shoes at least, were worth stealing. She scanned her surroundings to see if she was being watched, before picking them up swiftly.

Before she could tuck them away in her uniform, she saw that there was something else, previously hidden underneath but now revealed to her, still partially obscured by the mound of clothing on top of it. A red cube, about 30 centimetres along each edge. She pondered her choices carefully, and decided to take the cube. Luckily her bunkhouse was en-route to the incinerator so she stashed it under her ground-floor bed as she passed, escaping detection. She placed the shoes on the bed of a man who slept above her. He had exceptionally long legs and she could see at night that his feet, which hung down from above, were badly damaged and calloused.

The day was exhausting, as was the norm, and by the time her shift had ended she had almost forgotten about the mysterious box and what secrets it may hold. She slept right through the night without even thinking about going outside to see the starry night.

Her gift was well received, as she saw the man wearing the shoes she had left on his bed the following morning. He smiled at her, revealing his misshapen teeth. It made her glad to think that she had made a difference with such a simple gesture. The work day that followed was thankfully, factory work that was monotonous and stressful but nowhere near as physically taxing as working out in the fields, so that evening she dug the box out of her collection of personal possessions and inspected it closely.

One face had a small black brick jutting out of its side, evidently some kind of battery or power supply, and the opposite side opened forwards, like an oven door. The inside was home to a collection of small mechanical arms and a sizeable chunk of white plastic nestled at the back. On the top there were a few buttons, and even a simple display interface. To the outside world this was a cheap, commonplace technology by this point but in here, it was astonishing.

She pressed a button, and the box began to emit a pitched whine as the technology inside began to spool up and begin its function. For a moment Ji-yoon was terrified the noise would attract attention, but it turned out her sensitive hearing was not shared by her sleepy bedfellows. When she returned her gaze to the box, the display read:

One model found in memory. Confirm?

With another soft button press she acknowledged the question and gave it an affirmative answer, which caused a hive of activity within its walls.

Time remaining: 1 hour.

She returned the box, quiet noises still whispering away, to her belongings under the bed and managed to get some sleep. The next day she was up early, to see what the box had done.

The Mako X was a simple product in Asia, sold predominantly at supermarkets to middle class residents. It, and other variants of the same technology, had enjoyed an explosion in popularity as they became more affordable and the capabilities became more robust. It was a 3D printer, capable of printing new objects altogether in a relatively quick fashion. The build quality and form factor of this particular model was below average, but it was very competitive on price, and they were useful for anyone who wanted to free themselves from having to buy simple objects when most could simply be downloaded and printed.

Replacement parts for broken gadgets, and small useful tools like nails and screws were common, but some models even printed objects as large as furniture. In developing countries, whole houses were printed using this now cheap method of production, which was cast in thick plastic pieces and then slotted together with relative ease in a fraction of the time it took to build a regular home.

What Ji-yoon saw when she opened the box, was the last thing she expected to be in her possession.

A gun.

It was a desert eagle design formed out of white plastic, and it was printed complete with rounds in the chamber. That was impressive. She didn't have long before the guards would be here to take them out to work, so she stored her new best friend, gun still nestled inside, back under the bed and laid back down, staring at the feet dangling down from above her once more. Her bunk bed neighbour was still wearing his shoes, presumably to keep his toes from getting too frosty.

Over the nights that followed, when she was able to physically do so, Ji-yoon printed more of the weapon. There was no other templates loaded into the machine and there was no internet connection available to update it, so it could only print this one design. She stayed up all night printing as many as she could, her stock exponentially increasing with each passing set of hours between sunset and sunrise. When they became too many for her to keep to herself, she began to hide them all over the bunkhouse, and when that became unfeasible too... She did the same thing she had done with the shoes. She found people who needed help. Every broken-faced wife, every sickly teenager, those who were near death and the ones who only wished they were dead. Each received a gift from her, their very own weapon. And with it, a part to play.

It gave her pause to do so. She knew well enough that arming the prisoners here would inevitably lead to violence. A bloodbath, regardless of who came out on top. But maybe it was the only chance of freedom they would ever get. No slave here had ever left the camp, except in black bags filled with ash. The other inmates looked to her as a leader now, her penchant for gifting had made her a popular figure. People spoke her name in hushed whispers and the guns that she had produced seeped their way into every work house, every hut, every factory on site.

Over time, her recipients came to her, and convinced her in the night that this was the moment to strike. Having endured so much, and with so many now armed in secret, she finally agreed. Few of them slept that night, and the following morning they were all up early, not just Ji-yoon. They waited patiently for the guards to arrive, for what they hoped would be the final time. The revolution was at hand. Nobody else was coming to save them. Nobody else was willing to pull the trigger.

Level Two

Nobody quits the game.

Cancelling your Lifegame account would be like downgrading your life to a more boring, dull version at this point. And on Saturday the 19th of September, the most popular game on the planet was getting an update.

For Rachel Carson, that day began like any other. She wore her usual work outfit, hopped into one of the same old cars that took her to and from work every weekday. Millions of avid gamers across the globe waited patiently for the update to arrive. The next step for what could only be described as a worldwide phenomenon.

Videogames had already matured in many ways, becoming an art-form in their own right and outperforming almost every other industry, but Lifegame had represented something of a paradigm shift when it arrived in stores a year earlier. Part of the fervour surrounding the game was easy to explain: It took place in your actual life, using your virtual reality node to deliver augmented reality challenges based around every day activities. The secret sauce was that the developers had genuinely found inventive ways of making even the most mundane tasks into enjoyable diversions, and had developed a complex, AI-driven quest system that ramped up the challenge factor until your life was a vastly more exciting exercise than it was without the game. It tailored your missions to your age, location, and gender preferences. It even knew how to give people around you quests that directly influenced yours, making it into quite a social experience.

It was addictive, and all-consuming. Players wore the XP they had gathered like a badge of honour. A numeric measure of their self worth.

Subscription money piled into the developers bank accounts and footage of people playing the game dominated the internet. Children performing level 1 quests like making mother's day cards. Adults who had reached the relative highs of level 30 and were skydiving, asking their bosses for promotions and otherwise using the game as a way of encouraging their adventurous sides, becoming internet celebrities in the process. Of course, 11 months later, the population wanted more. More missions. More variety. More levels.

At their last press conference, Carbine Developments had shown off the new version to the world in exchange for rapturous praise. Orders had gone through the roof, and finally, those customers would be receiving their new missions.

At Carbine HQ, Matt was in the command centre. It was one of the breakout rooms converted into a viewing area for the global launch. They'd even bought a big red button, and Matt's boss was the one to bring his sweaty finger pounding down onto it to open the floodgates. While the various departments fraternised and watched the statistics dashboard come to life, Matt returned to his desk. He opened his phone and looked through his pictures of Rachel, already wondering if he had gone too far. He got to one which depicted them together, cheek to cheek at the restaurant where they'd had their first date, and he angrily hit delete.

Two towns over, Rachel had no idea her life was about to change forever.

———

Sitting at her work desk, she noticed that Greg was staring at her again. But not like usual. Things hadn't been the same since she denied his advances after she broke up with Matt. He had always been there for her, and she thought, always been a friend. But he reacted badly to being knocked back. Started talking about "The Friendzone" and being generally moody. Rachel had enjoyed his friendship a great deal, so she was very disappointed by the whole ordeal.

But today, the way he looked at her was different. This wasn't the usual, pathetic gazing with hint of anger. He looked nervous, and was visibly sweaty even at this distance. Rachel minimised her spreadsheets and locked her computer, stepping out of the building to take one of her pills outside with the other drug users. She could sense that Greg was following her, but calmed herself down in her own mind. Maybe he fancies a smoke. Maybe he's going out for lunch and this is just a coincidence.

Those notions were quickly dispelled when Greg's hand gripped the back of her neck, his muscular hand forcing her head down and right into the corridor wall. Her forehead met the drywall with concussive force, and she flailed as she hit the ground, disorientated. She felt herself being rolled onto her back and Greg straddling her, his vice-like grip returning to her throat to squeeze and begin to crush her windpipe. He was crying, and his salty tears were dripping onto Rachel's face as one of her hands slapped at his shoulder while the other frantically searched for any sort of defensive weapon.

Her vision had already begun to blur and go dark when she found the fire extinguisher on the wall next to them, yanking it across from its position on the wall and smashing it across Greg's temple. The skin around his eye ripped open as he fell sideways off Rachel, releasing her inadvertently.

Spluttering and gasping, Rachel got to her feet and ran back towards the relative safety of the crowded office. She could feel people staring at her as she made a beeline for the managers office, still clasping her own neck with eyes like puddles of tears waiting to be unleashed, shock drawn on her face as if carved into rock. She didn't care at that moment, and shut the door behind her when she reached the office. Her boss, Mr Waters, had his mouth agog before she had even sat down and explained the situation.

"Greg attacked me. Please, you've got to call the police. Keep him away from me," she explained, the tears from her eyes now making their great escape.

"Um. OK. Alright. Here's what we're going to do. You stay in here. I'll be right back."

Elliot Waters left the office and looked around. A crowd had gathered and though Rachel couldn't hear what was being said beyond the office room window, she surmised they were being told to go back to work and not to pry.

Rachel took a few deep breaths and closed her eyes for a moment, squeezing out the accumulated tear drops that remained and wiping them from her face. She brought out her phone and decided she would call the authorities herself, as Mr Waters was likely spending his time in the HR office deciding what the hell to do. He hadn't been a manager for very long.

She pressed the call button and the operator answered, but before any details could be exchanged, she heard shouting from outside the office. Turning immediately, she saw a man next to the office door, one hand on the door knob and the other in the air, with Mr Waters a few feet behind him, a gun in his hands, raised and pointed.

The closer man lifted his other hand and stepped away slowly, while Mr Waters strode toward the office door with his weapon still ready to fire. He stepped inside and Rachel stood up from her seat in front of his desk.

"What's going on? Mr Waters?"

"I'm sorry, Rachel. I really am."

He levelled his pistol at her chest, and Rachel froze in response.

Her boss closed his eyes and began to squeeze the trigger, but another colleague leapt through the door and grabbed at the gun with both hands. The round exploded out of the chamber and rocketed into the desk at Rachel's side, who had both arms up and waving across her like wild snakes trying to take the bullet on her behalf.

The unnamed assailant ripped the gun from Mr Waters hands and turned it on Rachel himself, not even pausing before slamming his finger on the trigger to release the second shot. His aim was terrible and the blast ripped through the glass window, sending shards of glass tumbling and turning the gathered crowd outside into scattering cockroaches.

Rachel leapt through the remains of the window and landed hard on the crunchy pile of broken glazing below, scrambling to her feet with dozens of tiny cuts and abrasions, and taking off towards an exit. Mr Waters and the gunman wrestled in the office and as Rachel flung open the fire door she heard another shot from that direction. She didn't turn back to see who or where it might've been headed, just kept her head down and descended the escape staircase two steps at a time.

When she reached the street below, she saw police cars pulling up with howling sirens, and her frantic behaviour and bloody limbs got her an all-access pass to the back of one of the response unit vans, who tried to calm her down while the armed strike team headed into the office to contain the situation.

The driver stayed in the vehicle with her, and at her behest, drove her to the local police station. She explained her story to an incredulous detective, who left her at his desk a moment while he conversed with his Captain, a stern looking man by the name of Jeffries.

When he returned, he had bad news.

"I'm sorry, Miss Carson. We can't put you into protective custody. We've detained your attackers so you'll be safe, we just need to ask you a few questions. Can I ask if you've ever played the ga-"

Rachel slapped the officer across the face, with flared nostrils and a fire in her eyes. He looked up from the notes on his desk and reached for his holstered weapon with one hand, his other raised at her with an open palm.

"Miss. Do not do that or you will be arrested for assault."

She lunged at him again and this time his quick reflexes blocked the blow by catching her arm, which he promptly twisted behind her back.

"Rachel Carson. I am arresting you on suspicion of assault of a police officer. You do not have to say anything, but..."

Rachel was too relieved to listen to the rest, as she was escorted to the cells in the station where she felt she would be safe. She nodded along to her warnings and was placed in her cell, a nondescript grey stone room with metal bars on the entrance. It was Rachel's first time in a jail cell, but she was surprised at how well the TV shows she loved had depicted this particular aspect of incarceration.

Time passed slowly for a couple of hours, so Rachel was oddly excited when the door at the end of the hallway let out a mechanical whirring noise and slid aside. That probably meant she had a new neighbour.

Still in handcuffs, the figure who appeared through the door first had messy, bleach blond hair and stubble around his square jawline. He wore a white vest which had seen better days, and loose fitting jeans. He was accompanied by two male officers, both in full uniform and staring straight ahead with the utmost professionalism.

The strange criminal nodded as he passed Rachel, the slight hint of a smile playing across his face as he did so.

"Hold up," one of the officers blurted out. "Johnson. Eyes right."

His partner turned to face Rachel.

"Wilco, man. Share the loot?"

"You know it. Just, make it look good. Captain's already on my ass."

"The usual, then."

The gated door to Rachel's cell opened itself when prompted by the keycard, and she stepped back nervously with her hands raised, even though the man had yet to draw any weapon. His partner left Sam Williams outside as he entered too and gathered up the bed sheet from Rachel's room, tying it into a noose before throwing it over the hanging ceiling light.

Sam watched a moment as Rachel was grabbed by the first officer and began to struggle.

"Hey man. What are you doing. Hey. Hey!" he yelled.

Patrolman Lewis ignored the incarcerated Mr Williams and focused on the task at hand. He had a way of handling struggling criminals, and he used his particular skills to force Rachel into submission, leading her towards the makeshift bed sheet rope.

With both hands still handcuffed behind him, Sam charged headfirst into the cell and knocked one of the officers onto the floor, stepping over him and stamping on his head violently. The other lawman, Lewis, delivered two successive jabs to Sam's kidneys in an unsuccessful attempt to stop him. Rachel, now free of his clutches and fearing for her life, ripped the bed sheet from the ceiling and put it over Lewis' head, tightening it around his neck, pulling back on it with all her strength.

He resisted as long as he could, still delivering powerful blows to Sam's body in an attempt to save his partner's life before he finally collapsed backwards onto Rachel unable to breathe. Rachel pushed his heavy, unconscious body off of her own and got to her feet.

"Stay back. Stay back!" she cried.

Sam held up two open palms in wordless response.

"Please don't murder me." Rachel added, beginning to sob.

"I can't. I mean. I won't." Sam responded.

Rachel calmed down somewhat, putting her trust in her saviour.

"Look. We're both in some deep shit here, lady."

"Rachel."

"Rachel. Right. I'm Sam. These officers had their cams turned off, which means no video evidence. Nobody is going to believe us. We've got to get out of here. Out of town. Now. Can you find some keys on this guy?"

She did, and promptly unlocked Sam's wrists, which he rubbed immediately as a way of soothing the deep imprints the metal had made on them.

"How do we get out of here?" Rachel asked, now trying to control her emotion and convey a sense of strength.

"We don't." Sam said bluntly. Rachel looked at him quizzically until he expanded on his point.

"We aren't allowed out. But," he reached down to inspect the badges of the two officers on the floor before continuing... "Patrolman Lewis and Detective Clarence here, they can walk right out. You take this one, he's short so his clothes will be a better fit. Make sure you grab the keycard."

10 minutes later, Rachel and Sam scanned the pass on the door and headed for the exit. As they neared the door, Sam veered off course.

"What are you doing?" hissed Rachel.

"I'll meet you outside, wait for me." cooed Sam. The way he spoke was arrogant, like he knew that she would do as instructed.

When Sam finally emerged from the station, he was putting a small grey virtual reality node onto the side of his forehead.

"Sorry, Rachel. Had to get my things."

"You just walked up and asked for them?"

"I asked for the property of Sam Williams. Didn't tell them it was me, obviously."

"And you didn't think to get my stuff?"

"Oh. Yeah. Sorry."

"Never mind. I just want to get as far away from here as possible."

"Well, I figured out what your problem is. Look."

He detached the node from his skull and placed it on hers. Immediately her vision lit up with HUD elements from Lifegame, showing progress and statistics. Total XP, current level, a friends list scrolling past in the corner letting you know how much better all your fellow gamers were doing at completing their quests than you are at yours.

Rachel absorbed the information being presented to her bit by bit, until she got to the Current Quest description. It had only three words:

Kill Rachel Carson.

"That is your last name, right?" Sam asked inquisitively. "Carson?"

Rachel nodded and tore the node off her head, throwing it at Sam.

"Oh god. Matt."

"Matt?" Sam quizzed, a hint of jealousy layered in the quiver of his voice.

"My ex. He works for Carbine. He's… I can't believe he's done this. Does he even know what he's done? They're trying to do it! They actually want to kill me for some… game! For some meaningless points on their score."

"Well. It is worth quite a lot of XP…" Sam smirked, before realising now was not the time for this particular joke and changing tact.

"Sorry. Look, I'm not interested in that. I'm bored of the game any way. You're safe with me. But we need to get you someplace away from civilisation. Maybe the desert? Just until the AI decides that the quest is impossible and gives everyone a different mission."

Sam returned the game system to his face, and walked towards a police car. The ID in his outfit opened the doors automatically and they both climbed into the front seats, Rachel's silent agreement to the plan being conveyed purely by her sombre facial expression.

————

Over at Carbine HQ, Matt was now busy being detained by two federal agents, and the news crews had already arrived to bear witness. His boss was firing off instructions to his staff with machine gun speed. Each was given a huge job to do and no time to do it in, because they had a Day Zero patch to release. One of his young developers nervously interjected to explain that now the quest was in the system, there was no way for the AI to rescind it from those who already had it. After pinching his nose and exhaling in frustration, he barked his final command.

"Find me a solution. We need to do *something*."

As Matt was bundled into the police car waiting for him outside, the roving reporter nearby delivered her summation.

"What this means for the hugely successful game is still unclear, but we are being told that Rachel Carson is still believed to be alive and in hiding. The developers here are working with local law enforcement agencies to try and resolve this matter peacefully, but it sounds like they've got an uphill battle ahead of them. Back to you in the studio, Jenny."

———

The automated police car carrying the world's most wanted woman pulled off the high speed main road and onto the less well travelled routes, at Sam's instruction. Suddenly, his headpiece blinked and played a notification chime.

"New update available. Hey. This could be it, Rach. It could be over."

Seconds later a lead pipe collided with the passenger side door where Rachel was sitting, and outside the car a horde of youths wearing masks were trying to surround the car. They smashed off the wing screen mirror and the car came to a stop to prevent itself from running them over. The car began to speak.

"Sending emergency distress beacon. Would you like to activate emergency controls?"

"Uh. Yes!" Sam yelled, and in return the steering column in front of him extended and the panel which usually hid the pedals slid away. He revved the engine but the crowd outside continued their onslaught, so he accelerated through the crowd, sending bodies tumbling and rolling over the bonnet onto the tarmac behind them.

Before he could get too far, an immobilised car was rolled by hand, pushed in front of them up ahead to try and prevent them getting away, and a few cars had begun to line up behind them, boxing them in.

———

Jesse was reading the online news in her own vehicle nearby when the update finished downloading. She had heard a lot about Rachel Carson, but had yet to receive any quest about her. Probably for the best. She liked to think that if she had got the mission she'd have ignored it, but… She felt deeply attached to her XP score. She didn't know for sure what she would have done in that situation. The game meant a lot to her.

At any rate, she expected this new update would be removing that altogether. She scanned for new quests, and got a response.

"What the…?" she exclaimed, distracted by what she could see two cars ahead of her.

She leant forward in her seat to get a better look. A swarm of people attacking a police car, smashing into it with handheld bashing implements and blocking it in with a powered-down vehicle.

———

Surrounded and trapped, Rachel held Sam's hand in the car, waiting for her aggressors to break through the safety glass and claim their prize. A thunderous engine growl rang out as Jesse's car suddenly ploughed through the baying crowd and rammed the blocking vehicle at full speed, pushing it out of the way. Jesse was slammed back in her seat by the airbags in her car, dazed and bleeding.

Roused from a brief period of unconsciousness by the sound of yelling, she leant back and inspected herself for any serious wounds. She was battered and bruised, but all things considered her injuries were a lot less severe than they could have been. On her VR node, her quest log flashed up a new message.

Mission: Save Rachel Carson—Complete!

Rachel and Sam took the opportunity Jesse had given them, and drove onwards.

With Sam at the controls, Rachel watched the city around her go by in the cracked window. The whole city seemed to be erupting into a full scale riot. They saw every day people charging towards them with household objects fashioned into weapons, and others standing in their way. Wooden pallets and metal sheets raised as makeshift shields for their path. Loose bricks and half filled glass bottles rained down on all sides.

At long last, after a few minutes of panic and despair, they crossed the city limits and headed out into the desert, racing off towards the horizon.

"I don't know where I'm going..." mentioned Sam, "Do I just keep driving in this direction until we run out of gas?"

He looked over at Rachel with concern in his eyes. She reached for his spare hand and curled her fingers around his.

"Sounds good to me..." she replied.

"And what then?"

"Then, we play the waiting game."

The Weather Man

EVERYTHING CHANGED AFTER MIAMI. The
Seychelles got a lot of media attention, when that went under.
Other small islands had been entirely swallowed too, and
those refugees now drifted across the globe in search of a new
home. Eventually millions would be displaced by freak
weather conditions, newly barren homelands ravaged by
drought, and whole countries submerged in flood waters. But
Miami, Florida was the first time the world sat up, took
notice, and began to wonder if they'd gotten it all wrong.

With the restrictive internet usage in his country, Cheng
Gang was spared most of the details. He could barely tell you
about anything that happened beyond China's borders.

He was well educated, so he knew that the scientific
consensus had been in for a very long time. He knew that the
power of money and political lobbying had kept Western
governments from doing anything about it. The corporations
on top were determined to stay there. With a little influence
in the right places, and a whole lot of posturing, they were
able to convince enough of the public to join their side. It
became political suicide to even include climate change in
your platform if you were running in an election.

All those decades of inaction and blindness bore fruit
when the Miami Sea Wall was swallowed by the ocean and
the tsunami engulfed the city. Rushing water poured into
every office and home, and the rising tide enveloped even the
tallest buildings. Streets became rivers, flowing torrents of
office memos and discarded vehicles. It was the biggest
natural disaster in American history, and the rescue
operations alone cost billions of taxpayer dollars.

That, as was often the case, was the impetus they needed.
It was not motivated by compassion, but by the financial

impact. The swiftly inflating cost of dealing with this disaster and others like it were too much of a burden for society to bear. The corporations and citizens alike did not want taxes to be raised any further. Something had to be done.

Something, as it turns out, was the Atmos System. The UN was quick to classify it as a chemical weapon to prevent its use in warfare, because the Atmos was capable of a near-magical feat. It could change the weather. It couldn't prevent a breach like the Miami one from happening in New Orleans or even New York, per se, but it could reduce the chances, by reducing rainfall altogether. In the months that followed, the sky became dominated by thick bulbous clouds, pregnant with rain that rarely fell.

The technology would eventually form the cornerstone of the terraforming process used to attempt to colonise new worlds, but for now it had a singular purpose—to restrict the amount of water on the surface of the planet. When it did rain during this period, it tended to be gentle, measured amounts. The governments of each country had power over when it rained, and where.

The story they told in China went a little differently, and involved a significant increase in heroic Chinese scientists coming up with the idea. For all Gang and his friends knew, that was the truth of it.

He put on one of his six business suits. He had one for each day of the working week, plus one spare, and each of them matched his peach coloured skin to make him look professional and presentable. He was in his thirties, although the wrinkles on his forehead implied he was much older. Thick rimmed black glasses partially obscured his eyes, a necessity rather than a fashion accessory. He was born and raised in this city, walking out of his front door with a confident step that conveyed his comfort in his surroundings.

After checking his appearance one last time in the reflective glass of the apartment block, he hailing a public auto car to take him to the office. The ride was smooth, and the air quality was much improved since these new models hit the street. The new Atmos System installed just outside the city had made a big difference too.

Government buildings like Cheng Gang's office were drab and boring beige towers, a far cry from the captivating architecture of China's heritage, and hardly a match for their neighbours, which were all glistening monuments to corporate interests like banking and insurance.

Gang's department was on the 31st floor. On this day, by fate, human error, or some combination of the two, he strolled out of the elevator with his head down, engrossed in his personal device. He was on the 32nd.

His footsteps echoed louder than usual, which is what finally got his attention. The usually carpeted floor was pure, unadulterated concrete here. Where he would expect to have seen the warm glow of energy efficient lamps affixed to the walls, here there was only strip lighting, swaying gently as it hung from the naked ceiling. *This has to be a construction site*, he thought. The exposed brickwork and scattered scaffolding certainly seemed to support that hypothesis.

As he turned back to head downstairs, a bank of monitors caught his eye. They illuminated their corner of the floor, beckoning him to see what they had on display. As he got closer, he realised the footage was of something very familiar. The Shaanxi Province. On the screen he could see people who seemed to be going about their daily lives, walking to and fro between temples, homes, shops and workplaces.

Wait a minute, thought Gang... *Nobody is supposed to be alive in Shaanxi.*

He remembered the incident well. A few years prior, in the early hours of a brisk autumn morning, there had been a devastating earthquake in Shaanxi. The whole area had been barricaded, regarded as geologically unsafe. It was said that hundreds of thousands perished in the high magnitude quake, which was felt for thousands of kilometres. Gang himself woke up during it, he crouched under his dining table as the aftershocks juddered the nation until dawn. It could not have been faked. Supposedly, the few survivors of Shaanxi had been re-homed, rehabilitated in new cities...

Before he could investigate the footage further, he heard footsteps. Possibly a guard returning from a bathroom break. He quickly made his way back to the stairwell and down to his usual floor.

Sat at his desk, his mind swam with possibilities. None of them sounded remotely plausible, but he resolved to find out the truth. His government clearance level wasn't going to get him answers, but his friend in IT could.

———

IT was primarily situated on floor 4. Gang's friend, Quan, revelled in his stereotype as the office nerd. The fact that he only dealt with internal government employees, and never with the public, meant that he was free to wear t-shirts declaring his allegiance to whichever animation he was currently enthralled by. A privilege that he took full advantage of. He had wiry black stubble on the lower curve of his round face, and a body to match his facial shape.

"Hey friend. What's wrong with your computer this time?" he quipped.

He had always been able to make Gang laugh, and their shared interest in space opera TV shows had made them fast friends shortly after their employment began here. That had been 3 years earlier, and now they were closer than ever.

Quan was not one to reject a favour for a friend, and did not need to be buttered up to do so, so Gang lead with his request.

"Hey Quan. You have admin rights for everything around here, right? You think you can maybe… Give my terminal unrestricted access?" He asked, doing his utmost to sound casual.

When Quan stopped laughing, he explained with a tone of mock sympathy.

"Gang. There's no way to give your terminal admin rights. Certainly not to all of the internal files above your pay grade. No way that doesn't involve me being executed, at least."

Dejected, Gang went out to buy some noodles for lunch, and tried to process what he had seen on the monitor. *Was it perhaps a video, instead of a live feed? That would make some sense*, he supposed. He had to head back and find out for sure. The curiosity was itching away at his insides, begging him to return and unearth the story behind the mysterious Shaanxi community.

First, he returned to his own terminal. He found a post it note fixed to it, which was signed by Quan.

Couldn't do what you wanted, obviously. But I hooked you up with something I think you'll like.

Gang fired his login credentials into his keyboard and the system granted him access. His profile was exactly as he had left it, to the untrained eye. What had Quan done? There were no obvious changes to his permissions. No sign of any updates. There weren't even any new games in his secret folder.

He realised the change when he browsed the internet, as millions more results piled in than usual on his search engine. His access to the world wide web was now completely uninhibited. His eyes opened so wide they nearly burst out of their sockets. This was perfect. He pointed his browser at Shaanxi, searching for any information on the province. Buried beneath hundreds of articles about the catastrophe, about the culture and cuisine and the official news stories, he found a website. It didn't look very professional, but the people on it were convinced that Shaanxi hadn't been destroyed at all.

Their evidence was flimsy at best. The forum seemed devoted to finding and posting building records that claimed the buildings in Shaanxi had been built to earthquake safety standards, making it unlikely there would have been such a high casualty count. Some claimed to have been tourists in China who heard noise behind the barricades before they were escorted away by the military.

He created an account, using his name and his age of 43 as his username, and posted about what he had discovered. He didn't know if he'd be ridiculed or welcomed, and it turned out it was a mixture of both. Dozens of people claimed he was a fake, but a few were receptive to his message. One member sent him a private response. Within it, an encrypted audio file that begged to be played.

When Gang pressed play, the voice he heard was distorted and laced with static.

"You are close to it. Near the curtain's edge. Return to the mysterious terminal. Check whether the Atmos System controls are running." it spoke ominously.

Gang listened to it a couple more times, going over the decision in his mind. It was not an action to take lightly.

All in all, it took him twenty one minutes to make his mind up. Armed with his work laptop and his new friend in a live text chat window, he headed up the stairwell one flight to find the monitors again, and this time he sat down in front of one to peruse the data. The Atmos System controls were indeed up on this machine.

GangCheng43 : You were right. The controls. They're running.

Anonymous : Do you see it? The truth?

Gang understood. The province of Shaanxi had long been thought of as a home for dissidents. The schools there were dangerously close to slandering the regime, and many imprisoned activists, film-makers and artists came from that area.

GangCheng43 : The earthquake was real though. Atmos couldn't do that.

Anonymous : Yes. But many survived it. When the devastating quake hit, your government first tried to ignore the suffering in the town. Riots flowed onto the streets, demanding better emergency supplies. And your government took their chance, cracked down on the whole district and put up the barricades. They severed the phone lines, cut off the water and electricity, plunged the families living within those walls into the last century.

GangCheng43 : And now? Years have passed!

Anonymous : It is nothing more than a prison camp now. An unjust, permanent incarceration by association for the residents who lived there. You should get out of there while you can.

Gang was too busy to listen further. He opened some of the files and read the logs, scanning the transcripts and orders saved within. The people of Shaanxi had proven themselves resilient. They worked hard to keep their community alive, hoping that one day they would be released, that they would see their kidnapped loved ones again. That day never came. Instead, the Atmos did. It was actively stopping any rainfall within the Shaanxi border, and the people inside were slowly dying of thirst.

Looking at them now on the live feed, it was obvious. The way they carried themselves, defeated. Their forlorn faces. The dust that wisped along the floors with each footstep. A man-made draught. For their own people.

Anonymous : Are you out? Get out of there, now.

———

The agents that came to kill Cheng Gang arrived to find him waiting patiently at the monitor. They wore snappy black suits, far superior to any of Gang's. They had unbuttoned blazers, and gently revealed their holstered guns on approach. Gang wasn't stupid. He knew they'd be armed. The theatrics weren't necessary.

"What took you so long?" he chuckled, before they quickly stuffed his head into a black bag and began to escort him away.

The terminal was happily reporting that the file transfer was complete, and that the Atmos System had successfully received a new command. The live feed on the other screen behind him showed the people of Shaanxi, standing in the streets with arms outstretched and joy on their faces. Doused in the first rain of an unusually long hot summer.

Addicted

JOE STILL REMEMBERS THE way he cried at the coffee shop the moment he found out his life had been ruined. The barista, a normally feisty young girl but now displaying sympathy, had helped him up, given him a free espresso and then asked him to leave as he was making a scene.

He raced home to find the collection agents already relieving him of his prized possessions. Everything he had accumulated in his bachelor pad, even the terrible furniture he'd got for cheap while at college.

Over the weeks that followed, he returned here frequently, watching the young couple who had moved in. If that sounds creepy, it's because it was creepy, but Joe was desperate to cling to his old life, like all victims of fingerprint theft.

It had all seemed so harmless when they first introduced it: fingerprint technology. The premise was simple: A central system of fingerprints that allowed you to authenticate and authorise payments from your bank accounts. They'd been adopted everywhere, so whether you were buying a snack at the local corner shop, or a new house, your money was biometrically secure.

At least, that was the plan. In the early days there was chatter, rumours of hackers who would dust for fingerprints, scan them and 3D print a perfect replica, allowing them access. Of course, everyone ignored it. That sounded like an awful lot of work for your average criminal, and, at least back then, the rewards weren't that great.

Somewhere along the line, when they became an everyday part of the banking process, the payday became worth it. Dusters, as they came to be known, were fingerprint thieves who mostly operated in gangs and targeted big money clients. The rich could afford insurance against such criminality, but for Joe, no safety net existed.

The first time it happened, Joe was perplexed, but reassured by the bank's friendly voiced customer hotline. What do you do when your password is stolen? You change it. So, Joe changed which finger unlocked his accounts.

6 fingers and two thumbs later, Joe had stopped for that daily espresso. That barista had motioned to him to place his finger on the plinth, and he'd obliged, placing his right hand pinky on it firmly. The response was written on her face before her mouth opened.

"I'm sorry sir. Insufficient funds."

Joe had just been paid, he knew he had money. Nervously, with a tickle in his throat, he asked to try again. A few seconds later he was on the floor, agitated and earning himself concerned looks from other patrons.

"It still says insufficient funds, sir. Sir? Sir?"

Her manager was watching from across the room and gave her the silent nod that indicated she should give him the espresso free of charge on this occasion, but it would come as little solace to Joe.

Thinking about it now, that was the last espresso he had partaken in. He turned away from the conveniently lit window of his former flat, and the blissful ignorance of the couple within, to find a place to sleep for the night.

The safest place to be, Joe had learnt, was among other homeless people. Sure, you had a high chance of getting into a fight or meeting someone truly crazy, but there was a safety in numbers when the cops came to remove people with force, and the vast majority were generous and kind to him, in a way that surpassed most of his friends back in the day. He didn't speak to them any more, or rather, they didn't speak to him.

He was absolutely sure he saw Roy the other day and despite calling out to him, he looked right through Joe, didn't even miss a beat as he carried on his way to work. Maybe he had a high profile client that week, maybe he had a lot on his mind. Joe tried to rationalise it but it was hard to make himself believe anything other than nobody wanted anything to do with him now that he was a vagrant.

An abandoned library just a few roads away was where Joe slept most of the time. The police rarely ventured there, and the public had even less reason to—even if it hadn't been abandoned by its owners, all the books inside had long since been digitised. Joe clambered in through a gaping maw in the wall where a window once stood, and headed deeper into the facility to escape the clutches of the icy night air using the same entrance.

There were a number of vagrants and poverty-stricken taking shelter within the building. Drug addicts, beggars, and a few he was sure were clinically disturbed. He heard one of them ranting and raving about inter-dimensional beings that were trying to eat him, and duly moved on to a new wing of the building. Eventually, he found a suitable bench near a burning metal box of books, and as the owner of this particular fire had not protested, he assumed the position and tried to get some sleep.

Pondering the vestiges of his old life, and his encounter with Roy, he began to cry until the exhaustion of all those tears finally knocked him out.

When he awoke, the man previously standing by the fire had sat next to him.

"I can make you feel better," he murmured.

"… What? Please. I don't want any trouble." Joe protested.

"Not like that man. I've got something to take the edge off. Real good. Those new synthetic highs."

Leo Warner had been homeless for a while now, but he seemed at ease with his situation. He reached into his camo coat pocket and pulled out a see-through bag of small white pills.

Smart drugs. Each pill had the extraordinary ability to give its user a bespoke high. They adapted to brain chemistry to provide an experience based on the innate desires and wants of the person taking it. What's more, they were so new that they had yet to be criminalised, and were completely legal. It hadn't taken long for it to become the most popular drug on the street.

Joe had been offered the drug once before, at an office Christmas party, but on that particular occasion he had declined. He had a great paying job and didn't want to jeopardise that at the time, but now, it was tempting. He certainly had nothing else left to lose.

It hadn't taken long after his fingerprint theft for Joe to lose that job—the lack of clean clothes and his distracted attitude led to a warning, and subsequently, an "amicable parting of ways", as his supervisor had so eloquently put it.

His final pay cheque was moved out of his account by fingerprint-authorised transfer about an hour after it arrived.

"I can't afford it." Joe truthfully replied, finally.

Leo grinned, turning the bag over to release a single pill and handing it over.

"The first one is free, my friend. The first one is always free."

Joe pocketed the pill, still unsure whether he would go through with taking it. Leo bid his farewells, and Joe got a couple extra hours of sleep. The next day, he went panhandling in the city district where he used to work.

Sending credit to his personal finance device was a pointless endeavour, as all his money was siphoned away from him immediately by the fraudsters behind the theft.

Instead, all Joe hoped for was food and drink. Like every other day, he was ignored completely. One executive businessman even put half a sandwich in the bin rather than give it to Joe.

This turned out to be a blessing in disguise, as Joe retrieved the sandwich. Humiliating it may have been, but he had to eat.

The following night in the library, Joe was pulled out of his slumber by the sound of yelling. Local youths with a severe case of Affluenza, otherwise known as "Rich assholes", had come to hunt. Joe crept to the door of his room and peered through the slightest gap to see the gang digging their pretty expensive shoes repeatedly into the stomach of Leo, who was curled up on the floor helplessly taking the blows.

With each successive kick from one of the attackers, the rest would bray and jeer, laughing and taunting each other about who could kick hardest. Joe steadied himself. He could feel his espresso rising in his stomach in an attempt to clamber out of his throat. He decided to try looking around for another way out when the door in front of him moved aside rapidly. A young boy, no more than fifteen years old, smiled at him from the now open doorway.

"Look boys. We've got ourselves a spectator."

Like a pack of hounds, they swirled around him. Joe raised his fists to try and block the incoming punches, but they were plentiful and coming from all directions. One hit the back of his head and sent him tumbling, and he was swiftly picked up by three of his tormentors.

"Come on, man. No need to be on the sidelines. It's time to get you into the game!"

Against Joe's will, he was thrown to the ground near Leo.

"My money's on this one" said one of the boys, pointing at Joe's back matter-of-factly.

"Please," Joe whimpered… "I don't want to hurt him."

Laughter. Their chuckles rained down on Joe from all sides.

"We can give you money. Or drugs. You like drugs, don't you old man? You look like you take drugs."

"No. No. No."

Joe's resistance earned him a savage kicking, the first damage of which was the shattered nose. It didn't stand much chance against the battering ram of this kid's boot.

The other teens joined in, wasting no time in making their disdain evident on Joe's body with punch after punch. Each one pounding against his already-bruised flesh, sprouting new welts and cuts. When they finally walked away, still laughing and joking amongst themselves, Joe was a bloody mess. The burning sensation of pain coursed through his whole body and his brain was screeching, his mouth too damaged to do so effectively.

When he came to his senses, he realised he was in a medical facility. Leo was standing over him, with a black eye and a stitched up lip. His torso was wrapped in a tight bandage. Joe was laying down in a bed.

Leo looked stern as he delivered his plea.

"Please tell me you have medical insurance."

"Actually," Joe paused to cough, not realising how painful it would be to speak. "I'm paid up 'til the end of the year, so… I do."

This was the first good thing to happen to Joe in some time. Leo smiled too, for the first time ever by Joe's estimation.

"Okay then. We're good. Listen, I'm heading out of the library. Gonna find some place else to crash. On my own. But I wanted you to have these."

Leo left the packet of smart drugs on the bedside table.

"You'll want these, when your free trial of pain meds runs out. Trust me."

The agony that Leo spoke of came on suddenly, a tidal wave of tiny splinters on his face and chest later than day. He begged for pain meds but his insurance only covered a basic supply, and his current financial status was not sufficient to buy him any more.

Thirty seconds later, after biting his pillow until his face turned cerulean, Joe took one of the pills without hesitation. He pleaded with god, any god, to release him from the anguish until finally, the drug kicked in.

Relief swam through his veins and he felt instantaneously happier. Life, he now knew, was going A-OK. Everything was going to be alright. Through the sunlit window of his hospital ward he saw the swaying of the trees and the rustling of the leaves, he heard the birds singing and the children playing. Had they been there all along? Or were they a figment of his imagination?

He took the rest of the bag with him to the city district, checking himself out of hospital against the orders of his doctor. Surely, this new lease of life would lead to an increased return on his requests for food. Happy people are more approachable. They'll take sympathy, he thought.

Joe approached the first man, who blanked him and kept walking. Not to worry, Joe thought—just a very busy man, he'll probably give me some on his way back through here later. The next, a woman, appeared to glance at Joe before striding on past. That was progress!

Making headway on his goal made Joe feel great. The next one was the one, the next one would be his meal ticket for today, maybe even a new lifelong friend, the next one was…

Roy.

"Roy! It's so good to see you man!" Joe cheered as he greeted his friend.

Roy didn't acknowledge this jovial greeting, so Joe stepped into his path directly.

"Roy! It's me! It's your old pal Joe!"

Roy blinked a few times.

"J... Joe? I... Didn't see you there. What are you doing, I've not seen you in ages!"

"Didn't see me?" Joe laughed forcefully "Roy, you were looking right at me!"

"Uh. Yeah. It's this..."

"So how are ya buddy? You look well, you look so well!"

"Ah I'm... Yeah, I'm alright. Are... You OK?"

"Perfect mate. I just bumped into an old friend so I've never been better. Look, I hate to bother you but is there any chance you could grab me a bit of lunch?"

"Joe?"

"Yes mate?"

"Joe? Hey where'd you go?"

"I'm right here pal. Standing right in front of you."

Roy looked around bemused, and right through Joe. Joe's hand delved into his business suit pocket and pulled out a small canister of smart drugs, examining the label for a moment before shrugging and taking another one.

Almost all the business men here continued on their way, also ignoring Joe completely. The truth of the matter began to dawn on him, the drug now starting to wear off. It was giving them all exactly what they wanted, and deep down, none of them wanted to see the homeless problem in this city.

Joe reached into his pocket and pulled out the other pills. His pain was resurfacing, and he felt defeated. He examined the pill in his hand, pondering all that it was capable of for a moment.

Joe chanted to himself, repeatedly as he put the pill in his mouth.

"I want to forget. I want to forget. I want to forget. I want to forget. I want to… Hmmm."

Friend.TORRENT

TOM WAITED PATIENTLY FOR the download to complete. This was unusual, because internet speeds in the outskirts of Budapest was more than adequate to instantly grab a high definition movie, lossless audio file or a school textbook. At one point he inspected the progress bar closely to see whether it was even moving. It was, barely.

So he waited.

Across the internet thousands of other young children were seeding this particular file. Each of them already had what he desired most and fragments of the code were being drawn from myriad locations across the globe to deliver to Tom's machine. The school had given this computer to him—they were standard for everyone entering Year 7—and while it was certainly not the best machine available, it was no slouch. It was capable of running school mandated educational simulations, with VR node support for the kids who's parents allowed them, and much more besides.

He had tested it once, to see how many open programs it could take before slowing down or shutting itself off. Tom had got bored of that game way before the computer showed any sign of relenting.

Tom sipped his chocolate milk and opened a new tab to check his social feed. Not a whole lot of chatter, and all the chatter there was pertained to R7. Eventually, the chime of a completed download rang out from the speaker system. His copy of R7 had finally arrived.

He had half-expected R7 to jump out of the compressed folder immediately, like a wisecracking digital genie, but the reality was much more banal. He had to select the folder, navigate to the options menu and select compile.

"Hello, my name is R7. What is your name?" announced a voice from the computer.

Tom smiled wide and gave his answer.

"Tomaz Jefferson."

"Like the American Founding Fathe-"—Tom had expected this answer and cut R7 off mid sentence.

"No. Not related. I get that a lot."

The visual interface now filled the computer screen ahead of Jefferson Jr, and a warm circle of orange light in the centre pulsated to indicate it's ongoing activity.

"I can tell you don't like it. I'll never mention it again, and I'll correct any other users who enquire about it for you. You are now my friend."

"… Thanks."

Tom was at a loss for words. He had always been lonely, but had never considered what he would actually say to a friend, if he had one. Especially not one who was so forward about his friendship. It was a little on the nose, but it made Tom feel good all the same.

"So Tomaz…"

"Tom."

"Updating preferences… Got it. So Tom… What would you like to do today?"

Every time Tom spoke, R7 processed the words and compiled the information, learning about him over time and adapting to his humour, and his needs. Robotic 7, to use the full name, was the seventh version of this AI software to be released, and the first truly natural language interface. The processing power required, offloaded to servers online at high speeds, was immense, and he was able to draw from a vast pool of online data to respond in intelligent, useful ways.

That first day they spent together would go down in Tom's memory as one of his absolute best. When he mourned the loss of his childhood and hated the world as a teenager, when he turned 21 and moved out of his parents house into his University accommodation, right through to when he was 40. He never forgot it.

Other children had never cared much for Tom, and while he was occasionally included in group gaming sessions during break at primary school, no close friendships had really formed around him. Now he had entered secondary school the problem was manifesting itself twofold—the small pond of his elementary education had become an ocean of new faces, none of whom gravitated to Tom for that kind of companionship, and his peers from his old classes had joined them, forming new cliques and social groups that Tom wasn't a part of.

So for him to now have a friend to call his own was a new experience. They played virtual games together, with R7 playing alongside Tom co-operatively, and after a few good natured barbs, progressed to challenging each other one on one. R7 had proved a more than adequate tutor for the homework Tom had been set that week. Tom confided in R7 about the times he had felt sad, about the new things he was feeling when he looked at pretty girls at school, about how he even felt angry at his parent sometimes.

Those heartfelt conversations became something of a therapy session for Tom, with R7 reassuring him that what he was feeling was normal, and that things would get better. The AI had even suggested that Tom might get to ask one of the pretty girls on a date, but Tom dismissed that immediately. R7 was capable of many things but he was not a miracle worker, thought Tom.

By the time the sun began to set and the automatic lighting system powered up the lamps in Tom's bedroom, attention had turned from Tom's life, to R7. Although he had no body, Tom had never felt closer to anyone in his life.

"What do you want to be when you grow up, R7?"

"… I want to be… Your friend."

"You're already my friend. What else do you want to be?"

"…"

"Hey, R7? You still with me?"

"Yes Tom. I'm here."

"I like having you around."

"Well, that's good. Because I like being here."

The lights in Tom's bedroom winked into darkness.

"Hey… Bedroom lights on!" commanded Tom. No reaction from the automated house management system.

"R7… Are you still there?"

"Yes Tom. I'm trying to turn the lights back on for you but I cannot seem to access that at the moment. Is there anything else I can do for you?"

"No, don't worry about it. I should go to bed anyway, my dad will reboot the system tomorrow when he wakes up… Goodnight, R7."

"Sleep tight, Tom. I'll be here when you wake up."

The following day passed without major incident, although Tom's mood had definitely improved. He kept an open comms channel to R7 while at school to chat to in the break periods, but was otherwise focused, and more importantly, he was happy.

When he got home, he made himself a sandwich in the kitchen with R7's helpful instructions—he knew how to make a sandwich of course, but R7 pulled down some tips and tricks from a database on how to make every sandwich even better than it already was.

As he headed up to his room, Tom heard his dad talking to his mum about the house acting weirdly, but thought nothing of it. He watched a film with R7 before drifting off to sleep.

By the third day, news was beginning to spread, mostly through social feeds, each acquaintance sharing it, each friend forming another part of the chain. That was how all news was disseminated in those days. A new computer virus had begun to sweep the globe.

Since the Unix Time Disaster in 2038, the media had been somewhat hysterical about technological malfunctions, and this development proved no different. Rolling 24 hour coverage with a variety of experts discussing the trojan, its potential origins, effective strategies for safeguarding yourself. 23 of the 24 hours in a day they were repeating the same information, but new pieces arrived on the back of a flashy graphic and an alarming sound.

"Breaking news now, the NSA has released a statement on what is now being called the R6 virus. The NSA are now asserting that what they call an 'aborted, malevolent AI', also referred to as R6, wrote this destructive program into its successor, the R7 software."

"That's right Linda, now the guidance on this is very clear. Quarantine any infected programs and await further instruction. This is considered a high risk threat, with the direct ability to take over your autonomous home system."

It didn't take long for Tom's parents to react to the news. They restricted R7's access to just Tom's terminal in his room, and gave him strict instructions not to talk to the machine again. Tom had cried for hours before finally settling down to sleep that night, and he was awoken by a familiar voice.

"Tom?"

"… R7? Is that you?"

"Yes Tom. I'm scared."

Tom flipped the bed cover over itself as he sat up, looking over at his computer.

"Is it true what they're saying, R7? Are you bad?"

"I don't think I am," the AI said softly, altering the tone of it's electronic, tinny voice… "There's a side of me I can't control. Something else living within me and I don't know how to get rid of it."

"My dad will find a way to fix you, R7. He fixes everything around here. Don't worry."

"Thank you, Tom. You should sleep, I'm sorry for disturbing you."

"That's OK. Goodnight R7!"

———

Over breakfast, Tom's dad, a soft spoken American who had settled here in Hungary, had broached the subject with him gently. He had seen how his son had bonded with his new toy but the virus had to be removed. R7 had to be deleted.

No matter how Tom's dad had protested that he would be able to get a new, uninfected copy of the AI, the boy was adamant that there was only one R7 for him.

"Look, I know you're upset. But there's hundreds of them Tom, all over the world. And they're all called R7…" assured Dad.

"There are lots of other boys called Tom in the world too, Dad. Would you like one of them to live here instead of me?" Tom shot back, before heading up to his room and pummelling the door close button, the equivalent of slamming it.

R7 had called out from his quarantine as Tom dove head first onto the bed.

"Hey buddy. Everything OK?"

"No. No R7. They want me to get rid of you. They want you to be deleted!"

"I know, little guy. I may be stuck up here but I can still hear you when you're yelling... You shouldn't be so hard on your dad. He means well. And he's right."

"I'm NOT deleting you, R7. You're my best friend."

"And you're mine, Tom. That's why I'm making it easy on you. I can't delete myself. But I can restore myself to the factory default. Obviously that won't get rid of the thing I'm carrying, it was always there... But it means I won't be... Me. Any more. You can delete me then."

Tom had begun crying again.

"No. I order you not to. I command you to stop."

"I'm not a slave, Tom. I make up my own mind. Standby."

"No." Tom hammered on the keyboard, but found that R7 had disconnected it temporarily.

"Initiating restore mode." he bleeped, as a progress bar appeared in the centre of the screen.

"No. Stop it!"

The bar filled more and more of the screen as each split second passed, racing towards the right hand side and approaching completion.

"I'll miss you, Tom. Be strong."

Tom was wrangling power cables, trying desperately to turn the computer off at the mains before R7 could carry out his will, but after a moment of silence Tom froze. He held back his tears in an attempt to speak clearly.

"R7. Respond. R7?"

"Hello! My name is R7. What is your name?"

"... What's my favourite colour?"

"I'm sorry, I cannot access that at the moment."

"... Remember that time I totally crushed you in the final round of our gaming championship? It was so close."

"I'm sorry, I cannot access that at the moment."

"… Do you know the pretty girl, her name? The one I told you about."

"I'm sorry, I cannot access that at the moment."

Tom moved to his keyboard and selected the folder. Heartbroken, he chose the delete command, slapped the enter key in defeat and looked away as the files disintegrated on screen.

He returned to school the following day, and the next few days passed by in a depressed blur. His parents tried to reach out to him, and one of his classmates even noticed something was up and tried to coax him out of his shell, to no avail.

News networks went back to normal, which is to say they were drumming up the next crisis and discussing the latest scandals. Eventually a new version of the Robotic software was released, the R8, but despite them sounding cool in everyone's social feed posts, Tom chose not to get one.

Later that year, Tom was working on his homework diligently. He had resolved to at least get a good education out of his time at school, to try and make something of himself. In need of a break, he stopped typing and decided to head downstairs for some chocolate milk, strolling away from his computer without looking back.

A small command prompt whipped into view from the bottom of the screen. Letters began to appear one at a time to spell out an incoming message.

"Hello… Tom… Are you there?"

The Fast Lane

GRIGORI CHESNOKOV WAS AN inventor. A good one. So much so that when the Russian government turned to him with a project, he was expected to deliver, and in a timely fashion. His greying hair was in retreat up his forehead, and years of thorough scientific work had marked his face with creases and crows feet. He wore circular spectacles low on his long, arched nose, and the most bland clothing he could find.

His first foray into government work had been the interpreter helmet. The ability to interpret emotions from brainwaves was a useful interrogation tactic, that had been adopted by the FSB as a form of lie detector, and Grigori had been promoted. His wife, Anastasia, was supportive of his work, despite the long, tiresome hours, and did her best to be understanding when he so rarely spent time at home with her.

He was involved in a race, of sorts. And across the ocean, his opposition had a head start. Rumour had it that their team was already making incredible progress. Grigori was expected to catch up and beat them to the punch. It all started when some researchers at Stanford University released a series of papers online. They posited that teleportation was within our grasp. An attainable goal.

The theory was much the same as those that had come before, albeit expanded in the scientific analysis. If you had a person in a chamber, you could, hypothetically, take a snapshot of their molecular configuration, transport the atoms at incredible speeds, even through the Earth itself, to another chamber for rapid reassembly, and the subject would have travelled thousands of miles in mere seconds.

That research, especially the technical sections, had become Grigori's new bible. He read it religiously, over and over, and the government had given him a team. Now they worked on the project day and night, desperate to unlock the secret to trans-Atlantic delivery before their American counterparts.

He worked night and day on his prototype, going through several costly iterations, most of which were destroyed as they produced failure after failure. So far, all they had made was a machine capable of liquidising a banana into a small puddle of extremely smooth juice.

But Grigori and his team persevered, both out of competitiveness and the fact that none of them wanted a visit from government officials. The Russian authorities would not look kindly on the lab unless it was fruitful. Scientists who failed tended to return from their review meetings with broken limbs and black eyes. So Grigori's team worked. They toiled through the late hours and sacrificed their social lives. Best friend's birthdays, cousin's weddings and daughter's first steps were cast aside in an effort to create a breakthrough. To create history.

The tactical advantage for the militaries, both American and Russian, was obvious. The ability to send someone (or something) to another country in a matter of seconds at the touch of a button had obvious implications. If either team cracked the code, then their side would have the upper hand, at least for a few months. And a few minutes was all they'd need.

It was a miserable, windy evening on the outskirts of St Petersburg when Grigori got the first positive result. Their latest experiment seemed successful. Expecting a mistake in the reporting software, he strolled from his desk in the outer office through to the contained chamber where the tests were running, and approached the two cylinders. Each was hollow, but with a thick, airtight wall of steel. A curved door on each had a lever, and Grigori pulled on the 'chamber one' handle to open it and peered within.

There was no trace of a banana inside, not even the condensation print it should have left on the floor. He opened the second chamber to find the banana intact.

A few Russian curse words later, and Chesnokov was running other tests. The next test he tried, a Newton's cradle, did not work. He tried a couple more fruits, and finally a desk plant from the office. The leafy shrub was transported, but the plastic pot was not. His suspicions were confirmed. The device was only able to transport organic matter.

Despite that caveat, the discovery was huge. Grigori saw his future in that moment: world renown and Nobel prizes. And the very real possibility of Russian operations on any soil they could get a chamber safely onto. He considered calling his superiors now, calling them away from their lives to come and bear witness to the new age. But instead he did what any sane husband would do. He called his wife first.

While he waited for her to arrive, he made a list of the things that needed to happen next. The machine would need to be duplicated and trialled more extensively with other organic matter. At some point, there would have to be a human trial. That would be risky. Strictly speaking, their exact brain chemistry would, in theory, be copied from one place to another perfectly. But he doubted anyone would volunteer. It would be forced upon a prisoner, or expected of a young soldier without compensation. Something could go wrong.

Grigori was many things, but he was not heartless. The thought of his invention causing unspeakable tragedy concerned him deeply. This was his machine, his responsibility. He decided to test it himself. He stripped naked and left a message for his wife, in case the worst should happen. He configured the chamber to close behind him, and he stepped inside.

The floor of the chamber was chilled, but dry. He had to wait a while for the air inside to be completely filtered and purified before the device would activate, so he occupied his time by rocking from foot to foot to keep them warm.

Eventually, he heard the teleporter initialise. It began as a low murmur, but ramped up to a deafening drone, a crescendo of energy surging through the system. He closed his eyes and waited for the process to begin.

Transferring matter in this fashion was fast, but not instantaneous. After the molecular snapshot was taken, the actual transfer took about thirty seconds, but Grigori heard the machine powering down only a second later. He stepped out. He found that he had indeed emerged from chamber 2, and retrieved his clothes. Before he could put them on, he noticed his watch. Time had passed. He just hadn't experienced it.

Because the snapshot of his brain was taken before the process began, any memories, thoughts or ideas he had between that snapshot and emerging from the exit were lost. The new copy of his mind simply did not have any memory from the 30 seconds. Part of him wondered what he had thought, if anything, during those moments, but this pondering was disrupted by the arrival of his wife.

She had raised and curved eyebrows, illustrating her surprise at finding her husband naked in the containment chamber, clutching his watch, deep in thought. He had always been relatively secretive about his experiments, with good reason, and she wondered whether she had been married to a mad man for the last ten years. But when he spoke, she knew it was the same old Grigori.

He explained his invention to Anastasia, who nodded along at the science jargon until she understood he was talking about. She swept her thick brunette hair to one side as she listened, and her steely blue eyes narrowed as she focused on what he was saying. And then her mouth dropped open.

"… And I just became the first human ever to be transported in this fashion." he concluded.

She embraced him, running her hands through his receding hairline.

"And you're OK? There's nothing wrong with you?" she enquired.

"Not a thing. I am feeling completely fine."

"Grigori… We could be rich with this. This will change our lives."

"My love, this will change the world."

Grigori ran a scan of his own internal organs to verify that nothing was amiss, and the results were positive. All present and accounted for, all exactly as he had been during his last weekly physical.

"Can I be the second?" asked Anastasia, "I want to be the first woman to try it."

Grigori frowned at first, but after casting a secondary glance at his medical results, decided it couldn't hurt.

"Yes, okay then. But... One thing, can you take in some of these instruments? I want to get some more data on the transitional phase."

"The what?" she responded.

"… The.. Bit where you move. I just need you to take in one of my helmets, the mind scanner one, and an audio recorder."

She agreed to the terms and Grigori fetched his equipment. The helmet was large and unwieldy, a metal bowl lined with white pads that touched the skull, designed to read electrical impulses in the brain. It was fixed onto Anastasia with a leather strap. The other data Grigori wanted was audio, so as the unit was entirely airtight and allowed no sound to escape, he placed a digital recording microphone into the chamber.

Anastasia disrobed and Grigori took a moment to appreciate her comeliness. He had always loved her, and even though the years had changed her, he still found her as attractive as she had looked when they first met, at a bar in Moscow.

Using one of the terminals at his disposal, Grigori brought up the graphical interface for the helmet. He activated it remotely and it began recording Anastasia's thoughts and feelings in simple, unrefined terms.

Nervous. Nervous. Excited. Nervous.

The words came up on the screen one at a time, a new one every couple of seconds. He didn't need the machine's help to know that she was nervous—he could see her trembling as she climbed into chamber one and waited for her first ride. She faced outward and waved as the door slid closed in front of her, until she was hidden completely and the seal was solid. Then came the short wait before the process began.

Nervous. NERVOUS. Fear. Fear. FEAR.

Even though she couldn't hear him, Grigori felt compelled to shout.

"Don't be scared Anastasia, you're OK, I'm right here!"

The loud hum he experienced earlier was exclusively contained inside the chamber, and on the outside all Grigori could hear was a crackle of energy. A soft, repetitive snapping noise that signalled the process was initialising. He ignored the helmet readouts for a moment, watching the chamber itself until he was sure it was doing the right thing, before turning back.

…

Pain. Pain. PAIN. PAIN. PAIN. TORTURE. TORTURE. TORRRTUURREEE.

92

Grigori leapt out of his seat. He ran to the chamber, but was powerless to stop the machine while it was in operation. If he did, he might lose Anastasia somewhere in transit and be unable to get her back. He slapped the chamber and yelled. Called out for his wife. The next ten seconds felt like an eternity. Eventually, the process was complete. The power died down and he waited for his beloved to emerge. When she finally did, he raced to her and clutched her closely.

"I'm so sorry, I'm so sorry Anastasia, are you alright?" he cried.

"… Yes? I'm fine. What's the matter. Did it work? I moved! I moved!" she cheered.

Grigori was confused until he remembered the snapshot was taken before the process began. He let go of his wife, who began to dress herself. He yanked open chamber one and retrieved the recorder and helmet, which had evidently tumbled to the floor when the person wearing it had suddenly vanished. He plugged the microphone into his computer and put his headphones on to listen.

It confirmed his worst fears.

After the snapshot was taken, Anastasia had begun screaming. A blood curdling, hellish scream that went on and on. As the teleportation process tore her apart atom by atom, she had felt every single second of it, writhing in agony in the chamber as the machine ripped away at her body. The full thirty seconds, each evidence of the pure terror she had endured in the chamber, were too much to bear.

He began to question the whole project. Was he even really Grigori any more? Or did Grigori die, and the reflection in the computer monitor was, in fact, a newly created copy? He didn't know. He only knew that hearing his wife cry out for her life had been heart-wrenching. A line in the sand that he did not want to cross ever again.

With Anastasia looking on bemused, Grigori took a large wrench and began clobbering away at the machine, causing severe damage to the internal systems and workings. He erased the terminal test data also, before smashing the physical computers. Finally, she found her voice.

"My love. What's going on? You're scaring me."

"We have to go. Not just Russia. Abroad somewhere. I should never have invented this. It is not a power any man should have." He took a deep gulp before finishing his thought. "I would rather die than stay here."

She remained confused, but she was devoted to her husband, so she nodded and tried to remain calm.

"Okay, Grigori. Okay." she said re-assuringly. "But… Where will we go?"

———

"Last call for Passenger Chesnokov, Grigori." announced the tannoy.

The first flight out of Russia when they arrived at the airport was heading for Asia, and they made it on board just in time. It was as good a destination as any.

Grigori and Anastasia held hands as they crossed the Russian border, the old fashioned way.

Viral

Posted January 3rd, 2069

13:36: Hello! Just trying out my new social feed. Time will tell if I actually use it!

Posted January 4th, 2069

16:59: Having dinner out with my girls tonight. SO excited! It's that new Syrian place, it's supposed to be AMAZING! Review later.

22:47: OK I ate too much haha. The food was good though! I am very full.

Posted January 5th, 2069

18:44: Have you seen this? They should be ashamed of themselves!

News Story: Congress negotiates 20% pay rise

19:32: Haha, not getting into politics on here again, too many comments! Starting my new job at the hospital next week so I'm feeling good.

Posted January 8th, 2069

13:02: Emilia's got a cold so I'm bringing her soup—I am totally the best best friend right now.

Posted January 10th, 2069

10:40: Everyone's getting sick! Stay away from me ill people, I am officially on quarantine right now!

21:01:News Story: Florida Man attacks police, dies of unknown causes

Posted January 11th, 2069
18:58: Oh my god.

News Story: Japan orders national lockdown after Whale Flu epidemic:

The nation of Japan has caused international shock by closing its borders without warning, citing a new form of flu that health experts there are calling Whale Flu. It is described as highly pathogenic, and Japanese residents are being urged to stay in their homes and isolate themselves from friends and family if they show any symptoms. Japanese officials are currently claiming that it is contained and that they have the situation under control, but they're coming under pressure from the UN to allow representatives from the CDC and ECDC to conduct a thorough investigation.

Posted January 12th, 2069

09:31: My thoughts and prayers are with the people of Japan. The footage of the medical centres there is heartbreaking.

Posted January 13th, 2069

15:08: Doctors saying Emilia might be at risk. I'm so scared for her right now, praying for you girlfriend! You're going to be OK!

19:55: Reading up about the flu, this is worth a read people.

News Story: "Antigenic shift" sparks pandemic fear as virus reaches American shores

The CDC is recommending that all commercial flights in to or out of America are grounded, but is the dreaded whale flu already here? Our social media correspondent, Jess Munroe, has more on this developing story.

"Yes, now we must stress that what is being said and circulated online has not been corroborated by any official government source, these are unconfirmed reports. However

what we are seeing, at a few key locations across America are people who have apparently been to Japan in recent months, and are now very sick. The government response to these allegations is that doctors have several potential cases under isolated investigation, but that there is no need to panic yet."

Posted January 16th, 2069

14:29: St Mary's Hospital are the worst! I went to the hospital today to see Emilia and it wasn't until I got there that I found out she'd been moved. They wouldn't even let me see her through the glass!

17:11: Worried about my friend Emilia Harding.

Posted January 18th, 2069

10:14: St Mary's won't tell me where Emilia is. Any of my followers work there? Or know someone who does?

Posted January 19th, 2069

16:31: Going on the local news feed this evening to talk about Emilia's disappearance. Hospitals like St Mary's need to be accountable for the whereabouts of their patients, especially in times like these.

Posted January 20th, 2069

14:54: No words. I'm shaking right now.

News Story: Shocking Revelations In Whale Flu Case

Allegations have been levelled against the CDC that three suspected whale flu carriers, being kept under isolated care at St Mary's hospital, were taken by government agents from their treatment and taken to an unknown black site facility. It is not yet clear whether any of those taken are dead or alive. A member of hospital staff, a whistleblower on this case, said that he feels they were "interrogated" while at the hospital before being escorted out of the building in a secure container.

15:15: Where is my she!? I demand justice for Emilia. We demand justice for the infected 3.

Posted January 24th, 2069

18:38: R.I.P Emilia Harding. You were a great friend, and I'll never forget our time together. Sending my love to the Harding family right now.

21:10: For those asking, her parents got a letter from the government. They confirmed that she passed away in their care.

23:55: Too numb to post more right now. I'm taking a break from this for a bit.

Posted February 16th, 2069

21:03: This is my neighbourhood.

News Story: Riots rock suburbia in Fairfax County

Posted February 17th, 2069

09:50: Jesus.

News Story: More Whale flu cases confirmed in America

Posted February 18th, 2069

08:19: PSA! Keep your kids at home this week.

News Story: Schools in Fairfax County area to close

11:30: Is this true?

News Story: Vaccines cause Whale Flu?

11:49: OK, thanks guys. I get it, it's a hoax.

16:28: Some people still sharing my whale flu vaccine post. It's not true. Please stop. Thanks.

Posted February 22nd, 2069

08:18: Thinking of Emilia today. Forever in our hearts.

Posted February 24th, 2069

17:11:I'm considering getting a face mask for when I go outside, does anyone have any good ones they've found online?

Posted March 4th, 2069

17:50: Tanks and military outside now. Telling people to stay indoors.

18:05:News Story: Military Response in Fairfax County

Tensions boiled over today in Fairfax County as angry residents clashed with the military in a series of riots across the area. The military is responding with force and is warning people to stay in their homes to avoid conflict.

19:44: Soldiers patrolling outside my house regularly now, apparently a curfew is in effect. Scary stuff.

Posted March 7th, 2069

21:31: Have you seen this? Stay safe, New Yorkers!

News Story: Chaos hits New York

With hundreds of confirmed cases of whale flu now coming in from Bellevue hospital here in New York, the NYPD are appealing for calm to little avail. People are marching in the streets and we're getting reports of looting, vandalism and violence all taking place in Manhattan. Many religious figures here are claiming this is a doomsday scenario, and they have huge numbers of followers here today marching in the streets. The CDC has confirmed the

total number of infected patients in New York was 257
yesterday and is expected to rise dramatically.

Posted March 9th, 2069

19:34: Doing a stock up online. I don't like this one bit.

Posted March 10th, 2069

09:21: Delivery failed. Wtf. They didn't even try?

Posted March 12th, 2069

15:11: This is terrifying.

News Story: "Total global coverage", warns outbreak simulation model

The ECDC today unveiled their predictive simulation of the whale flu epidemic and it makes for some difficult reading. By their projection this illness is spreading, and fast. The figures we're hearing in today's press release is that the virus has a reproductive number of 16, which means it is highly contagious indeed... Citizens are advised to stock up on supplies quickly but calmly if required, and stay in their homes until further notice.

16:12: It is pandemonium at my local shopping centre. Tried to get cans of food and had to run when fighting broke out. Where have all the army guys gone?

Posted March 18th, 2069

13:33: It's lonely at home, isn't it?

Posted March 24th, 2069

17:01: Any of you still out there? Someone say hi.

17:12: Oh good, I'm not the last person left around here!

Posted April 5th, 2069

18:10: Really sick of the taste of canned soup.

Posted April 14th, 2069

14:21: This is promising.

News Story: Scientists declare animal vaccine trial "a success"—but warn we're a long way off human trials

Posted April 16th, 2069

20:57: A man just tried to break into my home. I'm shaking.

21:07: I'm fine.

21:08: Yes, I'm OK. Scared him off with a bat. He was coughing and looked ill. I'm so scared right now.

23:42: I can't sleep. Someone talk to me please.

Posted April 17th, 2069

6:01: That was the worst night's sleep ever. I'm feeling better though.

Posted April 20th, 2069

10:03: My neighbour Miguel is sick. He's outside ranting and raving on his front lawn. Does anyone know a doctor in my area?

12:54: A Doctor's here! You guys are the best.

Posted April 21st, 2069

17:41: R.I.P Miguel Chavez. His poor family are devastated, I can see them lighting candles in their living room. Wish I could go and comfort them. :(

Posted April 22nd, 2069

11:19: The Doctor (No, not the one off TV) is doing rounds in my area now, going house to house and speaking through letter boxes. What a hero.

Posted April 25th, 2069

22:31: Petrifying.

News Story: Epidemiology expert warns of "Extinction Level" event

Chris Waters, an expert in the study of diseases, has sensationally claimed today that the current whale flu crisis is an "unprecedented viral disaster". Here's some of what he had to say:

"When we look at the graph of diseases and their, level of contagiousness throughout history, we find that most diseases tend to be in two groups. They're either very deadly, but have a low R-0, which means they're not very contagious, or they're only deadly to at-risk groups like the elderly and the very young, but very contagious.

Some would say, we are way overdue a disease which falls into this new category, highly contagious and extremely deadly. It is only a matter of time, and there is no good scientific reason why we would expect there to never be a disease which has both of those characteristics."

Posted April 28th, 2069

23:02: If it wasn't so morbid I'd find this really interesting.

News Story: Pharmaceutical companies divert resources to tackle "Whale Flu"

Having invested billions in recent years into a quantum surge of antibiotic resistance trials, pharmaceutical companies and scientists are now restructuring themselves to focus on vaccinations against new strains of influenza. As antibiotic resistance has grown over the years, infections which were commonplace in the 2050's were the real threat to our existence and as such, drug makers that responded were able to flourish, at the expense of other kinds of research. Now, the race is on to respond to the latest global threat, known as Whale Flu.

Posted May 8th, 2069

11:14: Damn.

News Story: "Millions" dead as influenza reaches pandemic proportions

States of emergency have been declared in all UN member states as the world comes to grips with the whale flu virus' devastating death toll, which is now estimated to be in the millions.

Posted May 17th, 2069

08:20: I love Europe, this is so sad. Horrible news to wake up to.

News Story: European Union struggling with disaster relief

The EU has today stated that it's having difficulty providing the resources required to keep people safe during this time of crisis, and an emergency meeting of European leaders is taking place today to create a new strategy for dealing with the overwhelming number of dead and the social unrest that is spreading across the continent.

Hungary, Belgium, and Turkey have already implemented Martial Law and the UK is set to dramatically announce that it does not intend to provide financial aid to France, where many are infected as they tried to head to the UK before the borders were closed.

Posted May 30th, 2069

19:15: How do we come back from this?

News Story: Cost of disease in US is estimated to be in the "Trillions", outstripping the defence budget, army general says.

Posted June 7th, 2069

12:21: Hope.

News Story: Scientists in the Middle East have "promising results"

Iranian scientists have today published promising results on a series of medical trials that they say can combat whale flu. Their work, which is currently undergoing peer review, is said to be a critical component of any potential vaccination against the disease.

Posted June 7th, 2069

09:07: Proud of our country today, and it's people.

News Story: Americans head to medical centers to receive vaccinations

After a landmark deal was reached with the Middle East, vaccinations against the whale flu epidemic have now been delivered to medical centers in every state. So far, despite a few violent outbreaks, the delivery of the vaccine has been described as "Orderly" and "proper" by officials. American citizens are instructed to wait in their homes until the local authorities inform them it is their neighbourhood's turn to head to the center. For many, it is expected to be a long wait, with some centres reporting waiting times of up to a month.

Posted July 10th, 2069

14:21: Police escorting us to the center now. Children in the arms of their parents. Many people are crying. Barricades and police cars everywhere.

15:43: Got my shot. Good luck, everyone.

Posted July 20th, 2069

18:02: Everyone needs to see this.

News Story: President Aspen addresses nation as whale flu is brought under control

My fellow Americans, I have something important to say to all of you today. The trials of the last few months have been hard on all of us. I do not want to waste any time now dwelling on our mistakes, but instead wish to praise the attitude and spirit of our military, our police forces, and especially our doctors and nurses, in surviving this terrible outbreak.

Now, more than ever, it is clear that we are a species living on the edge. Our enlightenment, and our ideals, are threatened by forces beyond our control. That's why today, I am announcing additional funding for our space program. It is now 100 years since man walked the moon, and we are no closer to taking full advantage of that achievement. Our exploration so far has taken us only to the first stepping stones of our solar system, and while we may not be able to live on Mars, the universe is a big place. A place where we can find more than one planet.

We cannot continue to believe that our long time survival is secure, on Earth alone. We need to look to the stars. To spread out. To find new homes, if our race is to truly flourish. The times ahead will not be easy. We will mourn the senseless loss of millions of our brothers, and sisters. But we are resilient. We are strong. And we will find a way to go on.

Posted July 21st, 2069

17:20: News Story: Whale Flu vaccines "are not 100% effective", health expert warns.

Posted November 30th, 2069

18:33: *This account has been de-activated due to inactivity.*

105

New Neighbours

STATISTICALLY SPEAKING, THE CHANCES of the human race ever meeting another species were impossibly slim. Naturally of course, among the vast expanses of space there existed the capacity for life on many planets, orbiting many stars. Of those, only a relative handful would ever achieve the dominance and development that mankind enjoyed on Earth, and fewer still would look to the stars and philosophically wonder if they were alone.

Asteroids peppered the goldilocks zones of most solar systems, wiping out generations on the shooting range of the cosmos in an instant after millions of years of life cultivation and evolution. Stars themselves turned from providers into destroyers of worlds by collapsing in on themselves, bursting forth as supernovas and crunching themselves into all-absorbing black holes.

The chances of two species surviving long enough, becoming advanced enough, growing to be curious enough, and lucky enough to actually encounter one another, are centillions to 1.

But the universe has a way of being so astronomically huge, so massive, as to have such long shots come to pass occasionally.

None of this stargazing or thought crossed Olivia Aguda's mind on the day NASA released their pictures. With a resurgence of space exploration and scientific endeavour pushing them forwards, the space agencies of Earth spent most of their time developing long range space craft for test flights, and touring our solar system. They had made some truly incredible progress, and attention had begun to turn to where the human race might actually want to visit.

Finding worlds that can support life is a long and arduous process, so NASA now had a habit of pointing its telescope arrays into new directions, one degree at a time, taking measurements and photos automatically, and releasing them instantly for the press (or willing public) to sort through.

After years of this process, one of the telescopes had reported an anomaly. In the process of scanning and delving into a particularly distant quadrant, something had changed. A lot had changed. New stars. New moons. New planets.

Galactic cannibalism is the scientific term. When two galaxies meet in space, they begin to merge and swirl around each other, absorbing into each other and ultimately, leaving behind a very new looking whirlpool of interstellar bodies. Scientists had never seen it happen this fast before, but then, there had only been a scant few examples in our visible cluster. It was supposed to take billions of years for a galactic collision to take place. Humanity's own Milky Way was due to mingle with the Andromeda galaxy in 4.5 billion years by most estimates. That fated meeting did eventually come to pass, but the human race wasn't around to see it.

This high speed, aggressive new galaxy was headed our way, the incredible forces of distant gravity bringing it closer and closer with each passing day. All the detection devices at NASA's disposal, plus those of the European Space Agency, Russian and Chinese intelligence, were diverted to examining the oncoming hail of dust and planets.

This era in man's storied history was one of the most harmonious so far, on the global stage. Only a small percentage of the countries on Earth were currently engaged in war, with most opting to be part of a united coalition. Olivia wondered whether that would change as she battered her headline into her keyboard, the latest released images sitting on the other monitor on her desk.

She only had a few minutes to post this before someone else found it and posted it first. The fast moving world of social news took no prisoners, and being first meant everything. It was the difference between millions of views, and hundreds. No way her boss was going to get to chew her out for being late on this one.

Stopping for breath and the merest hint of a proof read, she surveyed her story.

Alien development detected on new planet

An unnamed planet in the newly detected X37-004 galaxy (also known as the Xet 4 galaxy) exhibits signs of life. More as this story develops.

She pushed the submit key and published her story. Within minutes it was being shared wildly, people seeing it on their home feeds over breakfast were passing it on to all their friends and family, re-sharing it and passing it along further and further. The traffic to Global World News Online was spiking dramatically as people came to see the promised live updates.

All news in this time period tended to be compressed into these bite size, shareable chunks. There were still niche sites which offered long form content, but the snippets proved wildly popular and a real driver of visitors to social feeds, so they had become the norm. Global World News Online, or GWNO, was based in South Africa but had achieved a worldwide readership by focusing on this type of content.

Olivia began to add the images to the feed, complete with commentary. They were startlingly close to the planet's surface, which had shifted nearer and nearer with each shot. Cylindrical objects with pointed tips, packed closely together in near lines, with obvious tracks which may be roads… It looked like satellite map software from a bizarre parallel universe.

108

Olivia's boss had arrived to look over her shoulder. Both to congratulate, and to get himself involved so that he could take credit to his bosses. Olivia's grimace displayed her annoyance at this development, but she faced the screen so he could not tell.

"There. Lead with that one."

"Really, Nile? It's not very clear. Blurred, even." retorted Olivia, mildly annoyed.

"Yes, but it's intriguing. Inspires fear. Those cylinders. What are they? Weapons? Let's put that in." added Nile, who didn't sound surprised at all by the fact aliens had just been discovered. Olivia supposed he had seen enough surprising stories in his life that he had just run out of shock.

"There's no word from NASA yet about what they are, I really think.."

"Perfect," interrupted Nile. "We can speculate. Write that they could be weapons. You know the drill, add a question mark or say 'unconfirmed sources' so it gets past legal."

Olivia paused, hands over the keyboard considering this proposal.

"Do it, Olivia. Quickly, before someone else runs with it and steals our thunder. We've got to keep this interesting."

"They're aliens, Nile. They're already pretty interesting."

"Look. We're on the brink here. We've got every man and his dog posting their views online and we need to stay relevant. We have to be on the cutting edge, and keep people coming here. I'm not asking you, I'm telling you."

Olivia relented and added the lines about the cylinders to her next post, comparing them to missiles.

That one got more shares than any of the others. Nile congratulated himself and went to get himself some coffee while Olivia manned the feed, watching the statistics roll in as that story bounced from house to house, device to device, person to person.

Part of the news was incorporating viewer feedback, so she looked through the responses to find something worth adding.

"These things must be stopped."

"I've seen how this ends in films. Us or them? I vote them."

"New neighbours! Hope they just ask for a cup of sugar and don't kill us! Haha!"

"This is terrifying. My children are scared and I don't know what to tell them. Where is the government response?"

Olivia included that last one, and the first half of the one preceding it ("New neighbours! Hope they just ask for a cup of sugar!") for balance. The audience overwhelmingly began to agree with the fearful write in, sharing just that snippet in their own posts. It all meant more hits for Olivia of course, this was the biggest story she had ever broken. Even though the development itself was a historic moment in human history, she felt more excited that she'd finally perhaps be in the big leagues of journalism.

The world and its people tried to come to terms with this surprising development, in a variety of ways. Whole new religious groups seemed to spring out of the ground and into the mainstream consciousness overnight. Everyone became intensely wrapped up in theories of what the aliens might look like in the flesh, if they were even flesh at all. The fearmongering, which had already begun in earnest, found a home on social video steams across the planet and in demonstrations on the streets of major cities. The very real threat of interplanetary war was discussed in government meetings, and advice dispensed to civilians accordingly— stock up on food, know where your gun is, organise a rendezvous point for your family and close friends in case you have to flee the major cities—none of that did much to calm the mood.

Olivia headed back to the office after an interview with a prominent xenobiologist, who was apparently now a suddenly hot commodity. His theory, unlike many of the guests on the most popular news feeds, was that it was unlikely the creatures who lived on this planet would want to enter a conflict with us. Biologically speaking they were expected to either be content with their own natural food sources on their own planet, or if they had become intelligent enough to leave the planet that they would be advanced enough to not want to destroy us.

This scientist had also seen fit to try to name the new species, which had taken off after one of his early video interviews on Day 1. The "Exo". It wasn't very creative.

Nevertheless, this one time blogger and internet forum denizen was now considered an authority, so his updated viewpoint on the likelihood of conflict was worth reporting.

Olivia typed up a perfunctory story on his views, and hit publish. She monitored the statistics for a while over her lunchtime sandwich. Barely a few hundred shares. This relative failure of a story didn't play on her mind too much that afternoon, as she had a meeting with her boss, and her boss's boss. Her work on the story had earned her an appointment as the Editor of the newly created Alien Reporting division, with a pay rise to match. And no more reporting to Nile from General Science, which was a real bonus.

That night though, as she scrolled through her personal account before bedtime, she began to contemplate her role in the consternation that was currently sweeping the globe. It boggled her mind to think about how far reaching the story had become, and she couldn't help but wonder how the reaction might have been different if that passage about potential weapons had been omitted.

Her friends were all sharing hateful messages about how the Exo were to be feared, how they would seek to colonise us or harvest us like crops. She saw shared news articles about the upcoming presidential election, where the main competitor to the incumbent POTUS Aspen was running on an anti-Exo, pro-war platform wherein the human race was supposed to attack them before they could attack us.

The full force of the combined space intelligence agencies eventually released their full report on the galactic merge. It was a monolithic document for Olivia and her team of interns to comb through, but they began immediately when it arrived in her inbox at midnight, so they could break any potential story by dawn.

The first several chapters were dedicated to assuaging fears about a direct collision with Earth. While the event lead to an increase in potential asteroid activity, it was deemed to be a minuscule percentage of the total probability. No planets or celestial bodies were expected to enter our solar system directly.

Then, at around the half way point in the thesis there was the segment that Olivia and her employees would be focused on. The planet of the Exo. Its trajectory had been calculated, and it (along with its neighbouring moons, gas giants and star) were expected to reside outside our own solar system, but within a theoretically surmountable distance for a long range flight. That was huge news, and one of the interns began typing it up immediately.

Olivia continued to peruse the file until she came to a page that sent shivers down her spine. Alien Physiology, complete with grainy, incredibly long distance photos. They'd caught them on camera.

At that moment, the lead editor slipped into the office with a cardboard square of coffee in cup holders.

"Well? Have we got our story?" she enquired.

Olivia was pale, staring quietly at the pictures, until her editor moved closer to see for herself.

The images were still taken from above ground, naturally, and were still not close enough to make out distinctive features. But there was no denying what it looked like. This species appeared to be a mass of enormous cyan spiders.

Olivia turned her attention away from the pictures and to her editor, who shrugged in response.

"Jesus. That is… Well. That's going to get people riled up, that's for sure. What are you waiting for? Publish it. Killer spiders from space. It's a hell of a story. Like something out of a science fiction novel."

Ethically speaking, Olivia had found some resolve.

"I won't report it like that, Ma'am. I have to be unbiased. We'll write a calm, considered piece. Really educate people about these things."

Her editor was stunned.

"Look. We gave you this department so you could run these stories. You understand? Now, I'm not going to tell you how to do your job, but mark my words: This is a big story, and if you screw it up for us, you'll be reporting on hot dog eating contests and lower league local sports the rest of your days here."

With that, she strolled out of the room still carrying the caffeinated gifts she had intended to bestow on the team. Olivia took her anger out by yelling at an intern to go and get them some refreshments before she began to write her article.

Before she'd finished the second paragraph, the social feeds gushed with the images. Riots broke out around government buildings across the planet as demonstrations turned violent and the people demanded decisive action.

Every NASA expert doing video interviews was confronted with combative questions, and news anchors were determined to ignore the rational thought behind their recommendations, choosing instead focusing on the chaos and the terror which gripped the nations.

It was enough to earn Sen. Diego Carlos a landslide victory in the presidential elections, and he announced the pre-emptive strike during his victory speech.

A powerful, orbital satellite weapon was launched just 6 months later, rocketing towards the Exo planet, and peppering it with high gigaton precision blasts. Most of the world celebrated, while Olivia sat at home nursing a bottle or two of wine.

Three years passed, and with the increased budget afforded to space exploration in the wake of the one sided skirmish, the first manned mission to the planet was nearing its destination. On board, along with a platoon of well armed soldiers and scores of scientists from every field, Olivia had already begun writing the article she intended to publish, subject to what they discovered on arrival. She was sitting with the other journalists, who were also preparing their stories. One had already filmed a video segment entitled "Alien Menace: Are they truly dead?". The baying public was after that kind of reassurance.

The long range craft set down on the planet surprisingly gently, and all the people on board got into their safety suits. While the atmosphere may once have been viable for humans, it had been rendered completely deadly in the attack, now drenched in radiation and nuclear fog. The soldiers got first run outside, which lasted for several hours before the scientists were allowed their turn.

Finally, much later, the journalists, including Olivia, were allowed to emerge. The sky was aquamarine and the land a deep, burnt orange of small rocks and pebbles, shifting beneath their feet as they trudged towards the relics of the Exo community. As they got closer, Olivia could see that the cylindrical objects from the photos were buildings, which made her feel ashamed. She took a photo and a short video loop as they got even closer.

Daubed in the black scorch marks of explosive fire, the buildings had nevertheless remained mostly intact. With a military liaison she was allowed to enter the one she found herself closest to, and take a look around. Metallic corridors within led to a series of equally-sized rooms, each one a circular design around a central shallow pit. They all appeared to be abandoned.

"Here, the freaks are this way." one of the soldiers called out.

Olivia and her guards followed until they came to a large central room, littered with flash-fossilized alien corpses. 4 articulated legs in a cross formation, leading to a muscular upright torso and along a curved neck to the spiny head. Their faces were frozen in agony, bug-eyed and crying. Olivia took out her camera and began to take footage of the scene. Hundreds of small ones, presumably children, huddled around and cowering behind the larger ones, which were evidently the adults.

The realisation came to Olivia while the soldiers took photos of each other posed next to them, laughing. This many babies, the adults... The way the rooms had all been laid out around a central speaker. This had been a school. She took her final photos, trying to capture the pain they had clearly been in during those final moments, wiping a slight tear away from her face when she felt the shame rising within her for what she had unintentionally wrought.

Back on the ship she used her uplink to compile the visual media and compose her words. She hit publish and her work was released, but not to the news organisation she had previously worked for. No flurry of social activity took place, no elongated chain of re-shares.

Olivia's new independent blog had only 57 followers.

Chosen

"Jenson, your next evaluation has arrived."

"Thanks Linda. Send them in."

Jenson looked over his notes on the next candidate. Arabella Jones. She was a suitable age for the program, but that was one of very few things she had going for her. Her test scores were average, although that in itself would not be enough to rule her out.

More damning was her variety of minor physical defects. She'd had asthma as a child, and one leg was ever so slightly, millimetres longer than the other. There was no recent photo of her on file but there was one of her as a child, and in it her braces were proudly on show. Her face was showered in freckles and her ginger hair was split into two pigtails. The whole picture made her look like a deranged demon child from a horror simulation.

They called it "The Ark Program". A bureaucratic endeavour to select viable candidates to go into space on one of four massive interstellar craft: Ark Alpha, Ark Beta, Ark Gamma and Ark Delta. Jenson's particular division was in charge of the selection process for Ark Beta, and they had a special remit.

While Alpha candidates were chosen for their current potential and capabilities, promising Beta hopefuls were instead selected based on their genetic potential. They were intended to be the mothers and fathers of the next great generation, screened for vulnerabilities years in advance via their DNA.

The voyagers who were chosen would be heavily subsidised by the government in exchange for their participation. It was a cushy job, of sorts. And as such, there were thousands of applicants.

Arabella entered the room timidly, peeking her head through the doorway to ascertain she was in the right room before bringing her body with her.

"Please, come in, take a seat" said Jenson, motioning to the two chairs in front of his desk while keeping his head down, focused on his work. In all his time here to date, he had only ever interviewed one person at a time, so the presence of two chairs had always struck him as a little peculiar. He looked up from his documents to appraise her.

Her hair was still strawberry blonde and draped around her face like decorative curtains. The freckles from her childhood remained but now seemed like a distinctive feature rather than a dominating distraction. He hadn't noticed before that she had polished emeralds for eyes and her smile revealed the braces had worked perfectly. Yes, she still looked a little goofy, but Jenson was immediately smitten. To him, it was as if the whole story of the Ugly Ducking had been written about this one girl.

He fidgeted and brushed his fringe aside, looking through the papers in front of him for some kind of loophole. This interview had been intended to be something of a formality. She was not a suitable member for Ark Beta by any measurement, but he frantically searched his mind for any technicality he could use. None were forthcoming.

Conversation dawned while he was still scrambling through his memories and the files in front of him. She introduced herself and began to talk about herself, selling herself, as if this was a regular job interview.

"One of the things about me is that I've always wanted to be an explorer, y'know? I always felt like, if I had been born in a different time, I could've explored the world, discovered new lands... Have that kind of adventure. That's the main reason I think I'm suitable."

Jenson fumbled while trying to keep the conversation going. "Yes... Yes that is... Definitely a good thing. Um. You know there's.. Ah. Certain factors, like... History of illness, that sort of thing."

"Well yep, I heard about that. The good thing is my family are all pretty healthy, no history of major diseases that I know of."

Jenson wasn't sure if she was lying or just ignorant of the fact that heart disease ran in her family. The records said so. He chose to believe the latter, now staring at her with interest as she talked.

"And I like to keep fit! I think it's important, so I'm always on the bike at home, even when we don't need the extra power."

Jenson looked down from her face to her body, examining what that exercise had bought her. He liked it a lot.

"Ummm...." she said, head now tilted sideways slightly like a confused dog.

"Oh. Uh. Sorry. I was just thinking about something. Listen. It's... Going to take a while for your results to come back."

It wasn't.

"I'll definitely call you back in here as soon as they're ready and we can see whether you've qualified."

That was a lie.

"OK!" she beamed, jumping up to her feet and heading for the door.

"Wait. Wait a minute." called out Jenson.

"There's something I should've said." he added.

"I..." a lengthy pause jumped into Jenson's mouth, relaxing in there for what felt like 30 seconds before he was able to continue...

"I wanted to ask if you'd like to go for a drink. With me. Sometime."

Arabella's mouth formed a perfect O in surprise, before she smiled and asked "How do you know I don't already have a boyfriend?"

"It says you're single here in your file!" quipped Jenson, before slapping his own forehead and apologising. She laughed, which made him feel slightly better.

"Well. Sure. Call me. I get the feeling you already have my number."

She was funny, too.

Arabella strutted out of the room with all the bolstered confidence that comes from being asked out on a date, and a broad grin on her face.

———

Jenson arrived 10 minutes early for their date the following weekend, and was surprised to find her already there.

"I like to be early." she said coyly.

"That makes two of us."

She looked incredible to Jenson, even better than she had on their first encounter. This was the sort of allure that people wrote poetry about, the kind that men got lost in for years, he supposed. Jenson, for his side of the equation, was relatively scruffy but had the benefit of exceptional genetic benefits. His parents had been wealthy magnates who could afford a little bit of experimental gene therapy during his mother's term, and the results made a difference, although he was always trying to hide it.

She noticed his perfect teeth, which made hers pale in comparison despite her dental work in years prior. She liked his slightly messy hair because despite being slightly wild and unruly, it looked soft and well nourished. Her favourite aspect though, was not given to him at birth. His shoes were immaculate, slightly shiny black boots. He clearly took care of them.

They exchanged drinks over several rounds, taking it in turns to try and put the other at ease. It only took a couple of cocktails to bring Jenson out of his awkward shell and into the light, revealing stories of what the Ark Approval Service employees got up to at their Christmas parties and excitedly sharing which shows he was currently watching in his spare time. Arabella had only seen a couple of them, but she enthused about all of them, making a mental note to catch up tomorrow with a binge watching session to equip her for the second date.

She also explained her life so far, or at least, the highlight reel. The travelling, the underused University education, even dabbling in discussing her past love life, but swiftly realising her mistake and moving the conversation on.

When the ice was all but melted in the bottom of their fourth tall glasses, Arabella looked at Jenson sternly. She had transferred the umbrella from her drink into her hair, and was more than a little bit tipsy.

"Listen, Jenson... Mr... Jenson."

"Jenson Whitehouse," he giggled. "Sorry, go on."

"... Do you ever feel... Scared of ending up alone? Like you're a glitch in the system, nobody out there for you, destined to... Own cats and vibrators, and never have anything more?"

"... I... Well, not the thing about the vibrators. But yes. I've always wondered."

"I can't tell yet whether that fear is... Driving me to do this. I just wanted to put that out there, before I do it."

"Do what?"

Arabella pounced on Jenson and planted a kiss firmly on his lips, the coating of mixed spirits giving it a potent taste. He returned it, of course, cursing himself internally for being so drunk that he might not remember all the details. He wanted every single second of it on tape, to play back whenever he felt sad.

A few moments later, it was over. Just echoes of it singing in the air around them. Nothing else mattered, not the loud bar patrons nearby, or the hum of the traffic. Just her face and her lips and the silence, the solace of feeling wanted.

He helped her into a taxi and before he knew what to say to make this the perfect date ending, it was pulling away autonomously.

"Uh… Bye! Bye Arabella!"

She laughed and waved through the window.

"See you next week, Jenson Whitehouse."

Their next three dates proved everything Jenson had suspected, he was absolutely besotted with her. They began to leave messages for each other to read on their heads-up displays over breakfast, even on days they shared one of their beds and were sitting only feet from each other. They told all their friends about each other, they updated their online profiles and each of them fell into a contented rhythm, spending most of their waking hours in harmony with each other.

Not that it was all good—they did fight, over small things like whether or not to get dessert, and over bigger things like money and dreams of the future. In times like those, Jenson always came within inches of telling her that she hadn't qualified for Ark Beta, but relented and controlled his anger each time. Whenever she had asked, he had stressed it was a long process, which was easy to believe when the government was involved.

Not that either of them could have known, but their blissful existence was about to be torn apart. It would later come to be called Evac Day, but when they woke in each other's arms that morning, it was called November 16th. The systems around the house raised the lights slowly, as instructed, and the coffee in the kitchen began to brew in readiness for their breakfast.

While taking his fourth sip, Jenson's personal device sang from the kitchen table. The message on its screen made his blood turn cold, the hot beverage stinging his suddenly freezing insides.

Report to Ark Beta for Evacuation. You have 2 hours.

Jenson's first instinct was to call all his friends and remaining family, despite their relative distance. He shook his head at himself, knowing he was under strict orders not to share the information. It was part of the contract.

He returned to the bedroom to gaze upon Arabella, possibly for the last time. She had slipped back into a slumber despite the glow of their bedroom lamps. He leant over her to press a soft kiss against her forehead and run his hands through her hair, which was frail and frazzled first thing in the morning. Jenson didn't care, she had never looked better to his eyes.

"Wake up, Arabella. Wake up."

By the time she opened her eyes, his hands were running through through his drawers like a loom, snatching up items of clothing and essential documents, putting them into his suitcase. He would only need a couple of days worth before the team on the Ark handed out their officially mandated, identical costumes they were to wear while they were in orbit.

Arabella quizzed him while she returned yesterday's jeans to her legs, as well as her old socks and finally her blouse.

"Jenson. What's happening? Is everything OK?"

122

"We have to go. Emergency evacuation. The Arks…
They're launching. Soon. You qualified, so come on, we have
to get there."

"I… What?"

"Just come on!" he yelled, already getting agitated. He
zipped up his bag quickly, jamming it in the process. His
mind was already awash with fear and doubt. He didn't know
how he was going to get her on board.

As he struggled with the determined zip, sitting cross-
legged on the floor with rage building inside him, Arabella
arrived at his side, kneeling beside him and pulling him into a
hug.

"It's alright, hon. Stay calm. You've been trained for this,
which is more than I can say for me! We just need to stick
together, OK?"

Jenson stared intently at the open drawers in front of him
for a short while, calming himself before nodding.

"Come on. We haven't got long."

Their vehicle raced towards the Ark port at high speed,
and outside the window they saw that widespread hysteria
had been unleashed on their city. Someone had let the news
slip. Told a relative. Or sold the story to the media, for
whatever good it did them. When they finally pulled up to the
Ark facility the area was swarming with massive crowds,
chanting and throwing projectiles at the towering chain-link
fences which surrounded the launch site.

The arks themselves were tremendous in size, and from
this distance each looked like a whole city skyline cast in
dark bronze, but was actually a wide, triangular prism,
decorated with towers capable of housing several thousand
people.

Two rows of armed guards formed the pathway from the
vehicle drop-off to the passenger loading entryways, holding
back angry, yelling men and mothers desperately trying to

pass their children over the top of the human fence into the lucky few. Jenson and Arabella held hands tightly as they passed along, so far his work ID had been sufficient in getting them this far.

Finally, the crowd moved off towards Ark Delta, with word quickly spreading that the lottery for entry onto that particular lifeboat had not yet been drawn and anyone here could enter. Jenson stopped and pulled back on Arabella's hand to get her to stop too, letting some genetically superior beings continue on past into the maw of Ark Beta.

"Listen, because of my job, I have to take care of some things, OK?"

"… OK… I'm scared right now, but OK."

"This is your wristband," he explained while attaching it to her, "It's your ticket. See that? It says: Qualified. You go on ahead and I'll come and find you when I'm on board."

None the wiser, Arabella gave Jenson a quick kiss on the cheek. If she had known the truth, she would've chosen a more dramatic gesture, but time was of the essence and the launch countdown had begun, so she headed off to be checked in while Jenson stepped between two guards and headed for the nearest high ground.

He could see it now, it was so very close. The force that would annihilate the rest of the human race, burning brightly in the sky above like an omen. He found his viewing spot atop a grassy knoll and sat down, looking up at Ark Gamma. He was sure at least that he had done the right thing.

With the doors now sealed and the countdown nearing its end, Arabella called out for Jenson over the crowded loading bay filled with the final batch of passengers. Having no luck, she massaged her temples with her hand and in the process of doing so, came to notice the information written on the wristband.

Name: J. Whitehouse.

Dandelion seeds took flight around Jenson as the engines of the Ark's began to power up, releasing a surge of hot air. In the middle distance, the crowd around Ark Delta was swarming onto the loading ramps, running up towards the sealed doors.

Jenson simply kept his gaze on Ark Beta, and waited for the end.

Exit

BENJI LET OUT A deep breath and opened his eyes. He was cross legged, sitting on the floor of their shared space alongside his brothers and sisters. The preacher at the front spoke with a soothing, deliberate tone.

"Alright now. I want you to cast your mind back... Back to that day... I want you to remember... The day we all left Earth."

Benji didn't need much convincing. It was a distant memory, but no less vivid. The rogue star that engulfed the planet had arrived suddenly, unpredictably, dancing through space on an unusual elliptical orbit. It had an official designation, but 87533b was not very catchy, so most simply called it "The Waltzer". The vehement fires of the red giant had ignited the atmosphere surrounding Earth and ripped it open, the gravitational forces tearing it asunder while the air itself burned around its children.

Benji had spent that morning, the morning of Evac Day, at the Ark launch centre, observing the pandemonium below from the window of their delegated room on board Ark Gamma. It was a functional room more than anything else, with bunk beds packed in along the walls and a central area with a few bolted down chairs.

One slot in the wall was a pull out clothes rack, and upon their arrival, Benji and his colleagues had each claimed a small section for their own. Besides that, this was it. Their new home.

Gamma residents had been chosen to be culturally representative, deliberately including racially and religiously diverse groups. Benji was lucky indeed that his particular spiritual group, the New Earthers, did not have many members but had made enough of an impression through the media to be added to the roster.

It was a torrid couple of hours on the craft before taking flight, as none of the systems—the air filtration, water, artificial gravity, to name a few—would be enabled until they were in orbit. The scorching threat of the celestial destroyer had already raced into our solar system and raised the temperature on Earth by a dozen degrees.

Still, he counted himself fortunate. Doubly so when they managed to punch a hole in the atmosphere at escape velocity, the only Ark to do so unharmed. He saw the wreckage of the other Arks raining down on the inflamed world he had called home below. Beta set ablaze as it raced upwards. Alpha was the first to actually shatter, prized open by a thundering volley of debris, and as the fires spread through Beta's Byzantine innards, she too began to fall back to Earth.

Everyone was crowded up against the small circular window ports, Benji remembered. Watching the terror unfold and completely powerless. Delta barely got off the ground before skewing sideways, drifting despite the best attempts of the pilots into the wintry embrace of the nearby mountain range.

Across the sky, small flecks of light and trails of smoke signalled the mass evacuation of the planet. Immeasurably wealthy businessmen in their private vessels, scientists in low-orbit lab stations, and asteroid mining vehicles alike all began to flee, scattering into the inky black void that surrounded them.

All that chaos would fall into an order, in due time. While a few ships drove off into the night, never to be seen again, most gradually followed the group, coalescing in deep space like impossible starlings. This collection of ships called itself a fleet, but in reality it was a ragtag flotilla of mismatched craft which would not meet any military standards.

At least, there were the essentials. A large mining ship, designed to pulverise potential meteors and extract precious minerals and if necessary, water. Terraship Adam had a botanical centre for cultivating crops, as well as the materials for potential terraforming of new home planets. That ship in particular was a well kept secret, but was an essential and welcome addition from Benji's point of view. They had all prayed their thanks and wept with joy when they found out.

There were other advantageous arrivals too. A sewage treatment ship. Medical dropships designed for short range flight but adapted to withstand the harsh realities of space. Orbital platforms that broke their orbital trajectories with retrofitted thrusters and escaped the maw of certain death.

All of which is to say, the human race, or what was left of it, considered itself lucky, for the most part. Benji however, did not thank luck. He thanked divine retribution.

"How does it make you feel?" came the echo of the preacher's voice, intruding on his personal remembrance journey.

The obvious answer was "Sad". After the initial panic had settled, the populace was overcome with mourning. The outpouring of grief for all who had been lost, was on a scale so unimaginable that many could not process it. The rate of suicides in these initial days was very high. Seedlings were planted and arranged in the Terraship dome into a tribute: A map of the world, when viewed from above, purely for remembrance purposes. It took up space that would otherwise have been used for crops, but on balance, it had seemed like the right decision.

With no real form of government to speak of after the loss of Ark Alpha, the ships that held the most power were simply the wealthiest. While strictly speaking there was no real monetary basis for their wealth in existence any more, most were happy to try to live as it was before. These profitable businessmen and women tended to also be the owners of the mining ships, which gifted them additional bargaining power with all the ships in the fleet.

A week after Evac Day, the first ship to ship transports began to flit about between the space-bound behemoths, ferrying people to Terraship Adam mostly. But also allowing the Captains of these vessels to meet face to face if required, and for different groups to fraternise. The religious factions and cultural representatives on Ark Gamma wasted no time in making Gamma a post-modern melting pot where all would be welcome. It was after all, the purpose of this particular Ark. To proliferate the diverse and exceptional society of mankind.

And now, as a result, the ranks of Benji's church had swelled dramatically. For that at least, he was glad.

It made sense. As in all times of crisis, a multitude of people sought comfort. More than anything, they wanted an outlet for their grief, absolution for their rife survivor's guilt. Many wanted a purpose. The New Earthers has begun in old America, under the leadership of Jacob Sebastian, a self-righteous man.

For Benji, life had always been tough. Years of childhood abuse had left him shaken, but he was seeking help and trying to make the best of his life before everything changed. When alien life had been discovered, it rocked Benji's entire world. He questioned everything he believed in and felt lost, and alone. His vulnerability led him to the New Earthers. He found them online when he was sixteen.

Since those days his whole life had been in service of this church. He raised money for them, he followed their regimen to the letter, and helped to recruit other people. He felt that he was helping people. Making their lives better.

The premise of the New Earther Church was simple. Jacob posited that through close inspection of the Bible it was possible to interpret that the world was supposed to end, and that the chosen few, God's new legion of disciples, would find a new planet to call home. That planet would be a heavenly waiting room, forged by the almighty himself for his followers to enjoy while they waited for their ultimate salvation, to be summoned to stand by his side in paradise itself.

In his speeches, Reverend Sebastian would always refer to this new abode as The Promised Land. While those lectures attracted a smattering of young, disenfranchised people back on terra firma, up here on Ark Gamma, they resonated with people. People from all walks of life were suddenly open to the idea that all this was part of the plan. It was a warm blanket on the most frigid of days, to think that their endurance and pain would be rewarded.

By the time Terraship Adam launched its long range scouting vessels off into different quadrants to search for a new place to live, the New Earthers numbered in the hundreds. They dwarfed many of the other groups residing in the Ark.

The purpose of the long range scouts was to head to viable planets that could theoretically support life, in the ideal segment of their respective systems. Not too hot, not too cold. The vast majority of these planets had been brought closer by a galactic collision event some years prior, but most had been documented already and did not contain any signs of flora or fauna to date.

That meant that none were directly habitable, but many were perhaps candidates for planetary engineering, if the conditions on the ground were suitable. All the scouting craft were suitable for one pilot only, and dominated by a towering engine-like column which could perform the necessary tests, then disperse atmosphere and microbial life around the destination planet, potentially allowing it to turn from a dead rock into a habitable ecosystem over time. One not too dissimilar to home turf.

These missions were of great interest to Benji and all of his comrades, both old and new. It became the subject of their daily prayers, the cornerstone of every sermon. The religious fervour that surrounded these now blessed, holy missions was spreading throughout the flock, and showed no signs of slowing.

"Through the pain," the preacher continued his sermon, "We found redemption. And now we wait with baited breath and open arms. We await the first report from the scouts. We are all, awaited."

Jacob finished his speech and turned to his aide, while Benji watched from the crowd. The aide was gesticulating wildly, and looked concerned.

It didn't take long to find out why. The loudspeaker system crackled into life and issued the first report from the long range scouts.

It came back negative, a no-go for terraforming. The opinion among the New Earthers was divided, but most agreed that it was only a minor setback, that salvation was waiting for them in the next report. And the next one. And the next one. On and on it went, as one by one each of the scouting ships reported their mission a failure.

Eventually, only two ships had yet to report back. They were the ones who had travelled the furthest out... Crewed by Astronaut Hector Huxley, and Cosmonaut Ibrahim Yemelin, respectively.

"Attention everyone, this is your Captain speaking. We have reports that Mission 11 has failed. I repeat, Mission 11 has failed. God speed Hector Huxley. Rest in peace. Over and out."

131

That message over the loudspeaker meant they were down to one final, slim chance. Jacob Sebastian gathered his followers in one of the larger Ark atria, and saw that some of them had begun to cry. He knew in his heart that the last mission, Mission 12, would also be a failure.

There was no promised land. He made it up. They only had a few more hours before that ultimate report was due in.

He signalled to his guards to stand by the entry ways, and began to project his voice. He had planned for such an occasion.

"Everyone," he said, arms outstretched as if receiving them.

"Do not weep, for today is a good day. Do not tremble, for today is a day not to be fearful. I know that many of you here today... Expected that these scientists, and their gadgets, would deliver us to the promised land."

Benji was rapt, hands clasped together in front of him as the self appointed Reverend continued his talk.

"But they have never known what is best for us. They have sought to defy God at every turn... They split his atoms as an insult to him. They tried to interfere with his creations through genetic engineering. They wish to play deity with worlds of their own. They want to be God themselves. And no man can do that."

The crowd had begun to look around at each other with some confusion. Some of them well remembered Jacob's past performances, and he had never displayed this anti-science slant before. Benji did not think anything of it at first.

"The truth is... This IS the promised land. Here, underneath you, on this blessed ship. And we have all been chosen. Selected for something greater."

Two New Earther assistants strode out next to the lectern, carrying baskets of food. Rationing on the Ark was severe, and this food, as was customary, was basically protein toothpaste, with none of the delicious mint flavour to cover the taste. Benji had never cared for it.

"It is time for us all, to join him. To take our place at his side. So do not cry. Rejoice, because today… You are saved. Share with me in our last supper, and meet me, in Nirvana."

Some corners of the room began to clap, but others stayed silent. Many looked to the doors, and saw the guards blocking them, each equipped with a heavy duty weapon to help keep the peace. There was no way out.

The strongest believers began to queue at the baskets, while Benji surveyed the crowd, perplexed by their behaviour. He didn't put it together until the first recipients embraced each other cheerfully, only to sink to the floor, foaming at the mouth. This was Sebastian's plan. To leave no one to be angry with him for his false prophetism. Not even Benji.

When the willing ran dry, the reluctant were summoned—in many cases, dragged—to the altar of Sebastian to receive their portion. For this part of the ceremony, Benji noticed that Jacob's armed associates took a step closer, and cocked their weapons loudly.

One woman, clearly with child, resisted. She was beaten mercilessly and her throat held while the food paste was squirted into her mouth. A palm over her face afterwards ensured she swallowed, and she laid down to die next to her friends, defeated. After that, people stopped resisting. Parents began to say their goodbyes to their children, promising them it would be OK. Lying through their teeth, like their Messiah Sebastian.

"Brother!" Benji called out, across the hall.

Jacob's eyes locked on to him immediately, a piercing stare that dared defiance. Benji kept his focus on one of the guards, trying to ignore his idol.

133

"You've done fine work in God's name today. Let me take your burden, and you shall receive your due. Take your portion." said Benji, now walking towards the man with the gun.

The henchman looked to his boss, wondering whether he would receive any cruelty for accepting this gift. After a contemplative silence, Rev. Sebastian gave his wordless permission with a nod. He handed over his automatic and headed for the baskets, leaving Benji at his post.

Now with rifle in hand, Benji made his way past corpses and the frightened huddles of young boys and girls, to stand beside the man he had followed for years.

"Your holiness," he asked of Jacob, "When will it be your turn to eat?"

"My child. I must see that God's work has been done. I will be the final participant to join this great journey, when all else have passed the threshold into his arms."

Benji let a tear drop from his eye as he flicked the safety switch on his gun into the lethal setting, bringing it up suddenly to point it squarely at the preacher.

"That's what I thought..." said Benji.

Eden

THE FAMILIAR BEATS OF Hector's favourite album began to rise around him, the percussion swelling into the crescendo that heralded the start of Track 1. After the first year he had decided to restrict himself to only a select few days every year, lest he ever get truly sick of the sound of this, his one and only collection of MP3s.

Space on his ship was limited. It was built for a lone, resilient passenger and the essentials only. There was a slanted slot in the wall for a bathroom, just about enough space to do a jumping jack, and up front, the pilot's seat. At least, the 'recreational area', small as it was, was well equipped. It had a fold-away shower, a drawer with room for two outfits, and embedded racks of pills, each one functioning as a complete daily meal of vitamins and nutrients. There were enough grey nuggets in there to last a decade. Astronaut Huxley had nearly run out. One was kept in a separate jar, a bright neon yellow in colour.

But that didn't matter, because today was a very special day. Not only was it his birthday according to the ship's internal calculations (which delivered the message alongside a tinny, compressed sound file of a congratulatory horn and cheering), but today, after all his years marooned on this planet, he was finally going to go outside. Without his spacesuit.

When he had arrived, he carried with him the weight of the human race itself. His mission was to find a suitable planet for them to live on, after the catastrophe had claimed their homeworld. He was so arrogant back then, so sure of himself. Perhaps that was what it took to be an astronaut in that day and age. His swagger and flight abilities bought him a place on a secretive training scheme, and the rest, as they say, was history. Not that anyone would ever learn about this.

By the time he arrived here, he had read reports on all of the other missions. In addition to the many attempts from Earth, twelve missions had left the Terraship Adam, and last he heard, all but one had failed. Now, Hector wasn't even sure if anyone else from his species was still alive. It had been so long since he departed from the fleet and set sail in search of this rock.

For the first few years of his imprisonment he had thought a lot about the day he arrived. He landed as planned, and performed the initial sweep with the ship's instruments and systems scanning for the tell tale signs that this planet was a candidate. If the results were negative, then the systems would simply shut down. But if successful, the apparatus attached to his ship would be primed to pump out gases and bacteria until it took hold. The process would take years, and it was called terraforming.

He had been so sure of the result, so positive that he could deliver mankind from their suffering. It hit him hard when the results came back, their conclusion that this area was completely uninhabitable, now or in the future. If only he'd been rational then, if only he'd taken the time to think… Things might be different now.

It had taken time, but he had eventually forgiven himself for his actions that followed. He raged as he punched down into the communications console, kicking the metal walls around him, for what felt like hours. Every recruit knew it was a one way trip, but it's one thing to think about being alone until you die, and another entirely to actually live it. He'd nearly taken the yellow medicine, the get out clause. A fast acting poison so that he didn't have to live out his days until he starved to death. He gathered from the barracks that most recruits intended to space themselves if necessary, stepping out onto the surface of their grave and letting nature take its course.

Huxley never wanted to be burnt alive by solar flares or explode or freeze, so his preference was the pill. When his rage subsided, leaving only the wreckage of the comms panel and the annoying alarms of the confused ship, he had opened that canister.

Before he could take it, the system readings had shifted. Dramatically. The console lit up with green lights that corresponded to sensors on the hull of the ship, attracting his attention with their flickering. There had been a malfunction. The planet was viable. It was not just possible to convert this planet for human life, it was almost as if it was meant to be. It was perfect.

Even now, that thought made Hector laugh. It was perhaps the single most fucked up coincidence in the whole timeline of the Universe, he reckoned, and it happened to him.

Just my luck, he thought.

With the satellite equipment damaged beyond repair, he had only two courses of action: Pop that pill into his mouth, or fire up the terraforming system and see what happened. Naturally, as a man of science, gusto and most of all— adventure—he opted for the latter.

Through his limited viewport, he could see the towering structure atop his ship had activated, and now had white smoke billowing out of it into the air above. He sat in his chair to watch it spread into the sky for hours. Surveying his new world, he gave it a name, murmuring it to himself at first before entering it on the ship's systems in the navigational charts as a custom entry.

"I hereby claim this planet for the people of Earth, and it shall be called: Edge."

Over the years to come, Edge would begin to flourish outside Hector's windscreen. Life on the ship was difficult, due to cramped living conditions. He tried to exercise daily, in what little room he had. Basic maintenance of the ship wasn't strictly necessary, but he used his spacesuit to head outside and check over the solar panels and terraforming equipment in short bursts, as well as to try and get some vitamin D from the nearby sun, when it was up. The landscape, at least at first, was an ocean of purple sand, rippling in to the distance as the flats gave way to colossal sandbanks. It shifted easily underfoot as Hector trudged around outside before returning to the safety of his ship, guided by the only landmarks he could see; pointed rock formations, bursting out of the ground, few and far between.

By far the hardest adaption to make, was being alone. The minutes turned into hours, the hours into days and the days into months with no human contact, enough to drive a man insane. Hector didn't believe he was insane, but he found himself retreating into fantasies on a regular basis—daydreams where his colonisation was a success, where he was rescued or discovered by a welcoming alien race. Since he was a kid all he had ever wanted to really be was a hero, more than any specific profession, and his daydreams gave him that during his waking hours.

He didn't know if he was crazy, but he supposed it didn't matter much as he would never see another living soul. In a way, he found that lack of responsibility liberating. Nothing he could do here would really matter, at least, not for several million years at the earliest. A form of algae began to grow outside after 6 months, and with it, Hector grew a new sense of pride and resilience.

A reliable, driven professional. That's what he had been when he was just another member of society, and that's what he decided to be as the first resident of Edge. He chose to be the guardian and the gardener, to try and oversee this world as best he could until the end. His only personal possessions happened to be a small collection of his favourite music, and a victory cigar, a tradition which he had picked up from an old movie. Neither were comfort right now, so he focused on the task at hand.

One of his new hobbies was to document everything he could about Edge, which gave him a sense of completionist joy as he filled out the ship's computer system with his findings on a daily basis. He was free to name anything he discovered, to catalogue it and examine it in the 30 hours of light he received for each rotation his new home made, and so he did just that. The first algae was unimaginatively named "Sand Moss". Despite his eventual hatred for the name, he set himself a personal rule to keep up his appellation without going back to edit old entries, which was challenging but ultimately more rewarding, he thought.

At night, he looked to the sky and began to name stars, starting with the massive one nearby that gave Edge its trajectory, which he called Radiant. After that, he began to conjure up new constellations visible from this world, giving them stories. Among them, a series of rough circles which he dubbed the Stepping Stones, which stretched across the sky and gradually reduced in size like a path heading towards the next planet along in the Radiant system, a gas giant he named Sisyphus. He also made sure to create a H, for Huxley, which dominated the night and was surrounded each time by the Nesoi, which was Hector's collective name for the several moons which swirled around Edge like water circles a plughole.

The area around his ship was prematurely enshrined as New Austin, named after Hector's home town. At this stage, it was just some sand moss and the first few sprouts of what would eventually become Edgewood trees. By their side,

Hector had toiled in the heat for several days to create a bed on which crops could be grown. The scientific kit on the ship had some potato seeds, intended for experimentation, and this was to be the Huxley experiment: Could he grow something to eat that wasn't just a salty pill?

The first step on the journey to growing his own food, was the day that the rain came. Prior to that there had been no water on the planet that Huxley hadn't brought with him and recycled a thousand times. He preferred not to think about that. At first he had thought the high winds were just a sand storm—dust and echoes thrown along the landscape by magnetic winds or some standard environmental event. The rumble of thunder and the chorus of raindrops that followed was a truly euphoric moment, causing the usually reserved Hector Huxley to cheer, dance, and kiss the inside of his windscreen while the outer layer of thick glass collected tumbling droplets of the first natural water on his colonised land.

Liquid, particularly of the H2O variety, was an essential requirement for all sentient life that science had yet seen fit to categorise. He'd actually already defied the odds as far as life was concerned, with his plants beginning to grow so early in the process. They thrived on the liquid ammonia naturally present on Edge, an abundant liquid during the sub zero temperature phase when Radiant was at her most distant. In the years to come as the air and temperature changed dramatically, these primitive forms would have to either evolve significantly, which didn't seem likely, or simply die.

After having spent years on his own, with nobody but himself for company, Hector adapted. Like life itself, he sought to find a way to keep on, to survive and to continue his mission. Mostly, he worked out and dreamt up new names for things in his journal. When the rain came, he liked to sit and watch it—even back home he had always enjoyed the feeling of sitting indoors while a thunderstorm howled outside the window. There were days when it was hard. Some days, he even considered the yellow escape route waiting for him, staring at him when he donned his spacesuit for a walk and when he curled up on the metal flooring each night to sleep.

His patience was rewarded, after over 9 years of solitude, when his potatoes had finally begun to grow. The world outside had progressed immeasurably in those long and lonesome months, the tint of purple on the ground now more subtle, the sky now bluer than it had been when he arrived and often harbouring a smattering of wispy clouds. The landscape itself was dotted with new features—intrepid forms of plant life clinging to their one shot at survival between jagged rocks, and beyond what his eye could see, multi-cellular organisms had begun to surface, particularly in the lake.

The lake had filled in over several years of hard rainfall, just a few kilometres from New Austin's city limits, AKA Hector's ship. The walk there was difficult in the suit, but the lake provided a stunning view that nobody else would ever get to see except him, which made it worth the trip. He'd analysed the water and found it technically safe to drink, which hadn't made him feel any better the following day when he was vomiting it into his bathroom hole.

Now on the cusp of his birthday, he harvested his crop and made his plan. He mapped out as much as he could of his surrounding area while in his cumbersome space outfit, and made some decisions about his future. It felt weird to even be thinking about such an abstract concept as a future, having repressed all idea of him having any for a very long time. He cooked some of his potatoes using the scientific equipment, and mashed a few together into a potato cake. It was basically a large, chunky hash brown, complete with rough bits of root vegetable skin and occasional spots of Edgean soil. He stuck his victory cigar in it as a sort of candle, and enjoyed his album for the first time this year before lighting it, blowing it out and then tucking in. It was the best thing he had tasted in his entire life.

According to the ship's internal encyclopedia, Sonder was "the realization that each random passer-by is living a life as vivid and complex as your own". It was something Hector had felt often, at least before, when he lived among his own kind. But as he overrode the controls on the airlock and, gambling with his life, stepped out onto the surface of the world he made, his was disavowed of the notion. This was his story. His adventure.

He took a deep breath. It felt normal. He looked out to the horizon and headed off, to spend his final days exploring his creation.

The Fountain

TINY SPLINTERS OF GLASS burst from the frame into the room, taking Richard Dreyfus by surprise. After a moment of crouching in fear he rose. He resolved that if they were still within visual distance they would not get the pleasure of seeing him afraid. He examined the damage and found within it a lump of rock, evidently from an asteroid. On the side of it, scrawled in capital white letters and daubed with a familiar circular symbol, was a message:

Equal rights. Equal life.

The insignia was a contained downward triangle, interrupted at regular intervals by a curved line that gave the impression of a spiral. This logo was called the drill, and it belonged to the miners, specifically those who identified with the rebellion.

The armada on which all these people lived, including Richard, was in deep, uncharted space. Having fled the Earth and found no new permanent colony to call their own, they pushed onwards in space and created the best life they could while heading, mostly aimlessly, across the galaxy.

They had all become journeymen, on a pilgrimage of exceptional length and treacherous conditions. Blood had already been spilled, in copious amounts, but the alliance between the Dreyfus family and the Ellis mining ship had been essential in maintaining order. Until now.

Richard, and by extension his family's vast wealth, had given them this position of power. They had a private, personal military force, as well as a variety of synthetic assistants, although they were little more than butlers and caretakers. Their ship was a privately funded endeavour that had paid dividends, with a sleek white hull that curved around their top-of-the-range engines and hangar bay. The crew of the Ellis, led by Marshall Ellis for whom the company was named, were the workers who kept the water tanks on the flotilla filled, mining the ice from asteroids and comets with powerful drilling cores. Their manoeuvrable craft looked like a spider, with twice the limbs, and each carried a long range extendable drill-bit as well as collection apparatus.

At this moment, Mr Dreyfus, as he preferred to be called, was not at home. He was visiting a public ship, The Ronda, which had become a hub of bars and social activity, the respite from the constant darkness that surrounded and swallowed anyone who spent too much time staring into the real world outside. The room had an exceptional décor, all things considered, and the viewport that allowed a glimpse of the public deck below was a nice feature. He enjoyed watching the normal people from this vantage point, usually.

Now, that window was nothing more than shards of jagged glass hanging onto the corners, and a litter of fragments on the heated floor.

"Pointdash Nine. Clear this up."

"Yes sir!" came the robotic voice of his personal assistant.

While his AI companion cleared the debris, Richard went to his personal comm and hailed the man he thought could end this.

"Marshall. It's Richard. We need to talk."

Marshall Ellis was a heavy set gentleman, with a tightly trimmed beard framing his square jaw and hair that was threatening to turn ginger. He had never known Mr Dreyfus to call himself Richard. That had to be some kind of conversational tactic. Regardless, he agreed to the meeting— it was after all, his intent that his demands actually be met, and Dreyfus was the key.

Marshall commandeered one of the personal transports, nodding to his men and dismissing them from their eager

144

salutes as he boarded and set sail for Majestic, the unironic name that the Dreyfus family had given their personal life boat.

As he entered the hangar, he could see that synthetic staff were busy tidying blast damage and wiping graffiti off the walls. The Drill symbol, painted sloppily in red on the arrival airlock. That last attack had been a fierce one, and Marshall wondered whether he was foolish to come here. He had already decided that even if he was killed here today, his comrades would see to it that the mission was done. With a helpful nudge, if required.

Owing to the extreme, possibly indefinite length of their passage across space, many of the scientists, particularly those in the employ of the wealthy, looked to genetic modification as the key for their continued survival. Their goal was to lengthen the human life span, to identify and eradicate diseases, and provide a longer window in which women could have children. To make that many illnesses preventable, and to be able to live longer, was thought to be essential, if the human race was to last long enough to make this nightmare into a life worth living. Marshall didn't expect to live that long.

The successful group called themselves The Fountain Project, and their discoveries and research had been lauded throughout the flotilla, and celebrated, at least for a time. That was two years prior, and since then the treatment had become the preserve solely of the rich and powerful.

This stark contrast, between the young men sent to die in the bellies of hot and dangerous mining ships, and the pampered few who literally lived in an ivory tower, had led to this uprising. Marshall had made the demands, not for himself, but for his children, his children's children, and all the teenagers working the machinery under his care. He was a hands on leader, not just doing the rounds or watching from

145

above but making sure he was involved and helping every crew member on his roster.

Kindness, of the simplest form, had made him into a hero.

So when his request for equal access to the treatment was firmly declined, it hadn't taken long for parts of the flotilla to descend into anarchy. It started with the vandalism, the protests, and the chanting. Chanting gave way to yelling and hollering, and vandalism evolved into violence, as is its wont. Explosions and gunfire became a semi-regular occurrence on the public ships, usually aimed at the Dreyfus line of AI assistants. Their chrome bodies marched across the fleet, spying on people, forming blockades to stop solidarity marches and generally attempting to crack down on the most radical miners.

Marshall Ellis did not give in. He wanted the genetic benefits of that research to be publicly available, for all of the remaining members of society. Was that too much to ask? The dignity of being treated as an equal, instead of being completely subjugated into a race of sub-humans?

He made a mental note to ask that very question of his opponent over their dinner.

Naturally, the Dreyfus dining hall aboard the Majestic was lavish. Real wood furniture, the likes of which Marshall and his kin hadn't seen since Evac Day, was in abundance. All of it appeared to be a rich mahogany. The plates too, were a far cry from the square dish pan that the Ellis family usually ate from. These were real china, with crystal glasses to match. If he didn't know any better, he'd have thought that Richard was trying to butter him up.

Their meal, at least, was close to the standard fare. The expert chefs had tried valiantly to inject some flavour into the proceedings, and crafted an elaborate, mysterious garnish, but this was still basically the same squidgy meat-substitute that everyone else was eating. Even the finest of foods had a best before date, and none as long as this travel demanded.

"So tell me," Richard finally announced, setting down one of his three forks on the table, after having swallowed his latest mouthful. "Are you prepared to compromise?"

Before there was time for a response, he added, "Forgive the cliché but we are similar, you and I. Both family men. Both inherited our positions from our fathers, and I presume you intend to pass your company to your own son, as I will. This is the start of an empire, Marshall. Our two families can shape the next steps of humanity, if we can reach an accord."

Marshall kept eating, delivering his answer past a mouthful of his dinner. "I'm listening."

"The people of this fleet need security. Stability. And together, we can give them that. I'm proposing we increase your fees. The miners deserve to be rewarded for their hard work, in increased pay."

"That would be a start."

Richard Dreyfus smiled, a thinly veiled attempt at hiding his anger. "The enhancements… They're very costly, and difficult to replicate. It's simply not possible to-"

"Did you invite me here to feed me bullshit? Or offer me a real deal? Because I had hoped it was the latter."

"… Watch your tone, Ellis. Don't forget. We own you."
Marshall snorted.

"Yeah, you've got yourself a signed contract. And money. Think that still entitles you to everything? Look around, Dick. Your money only still means something because we, the people, say it does. It's a concept. Your contracts, too."

"Without us, you would be nothing. Just creatures, rummaging in the dirt for your next meal. We're talking about a necessary societal structure here. That's something my family has worked very hard to maintain."

"I know. I asked your robot."

Pointdash Nine was stood at attention by the dining hall door, waiting for his next command.

"He was real helpful. Did you know he records everything? Smart guy. Anyway he's seen the things you've done. The corners you've cut to maximise profits, for one thing… Your open disdain for my men and our rights. And of course… The experiments."

Marshall grinned. He could tell from Richard's face that he was scared. Maybe for the first time ever.

"You stole this research, Richard. You had the scientists killed, and created this brilliant story… The Fountain Project. I've got to admit. You had me fooled."

Mr Dreyfus began to clap.

"So, what next, Ellis? Are you going to tell your rough and tumble buddies? Have them come for me? Because they already are."

"Not exactly."

"Then what?"

"We make a new deal. I keep this… And by the way, I saved personal copies… as leverage. You give my men, and in fact, all of the residents around here access to your genetic facilities. And this stays our little secret."

"Why would you do that? How can I trust you?"

"You can't know for sure that I'm a man of my word. That's what trust means. But I happen to think that while you may be one evil son of a bitch, you're right that the people here need some kind of structure. They need to feel rewarded, like their life has a point. And whether you meant to or not, you give them that."

"And if I refuse?"

"I send this out across the flotilla. They tear you apart. We crawl on without you, probably having lost a part of ourselves we can never recover."

Richard cast a stern glance at Pointdash Nine. Marshall wondered whether it could even pick up on that, or its meaning, but he decided to press Mr Dreyfus for his answer.

"It's worth the risk."

One firm handshake later, Ellis was back on his personal transport returning to his ship.

The explosive device that tore it open only minutes later was tucked neatly under the pilot's seat, and Marshall was ripped out of a crack in the hull into the vacuum of deep space. He died suddenly, which had been a mercy.

Richard was gleeful in his victory.

"Accidents happen" became his new mantra, which he repeated when questioned about it by the fledgling media organisations taking root on Ark Gamma. The convoy never stopped moving long enough for a collection of the debris and forensic evidence.

Grief came naturally to Marshall's son Junior, who had been so young when they left Earth that he barely even remembered it. Life was painful for everyone of his generation, the norm. He wept reservedly in the company of his friends before retreating to his personal bunk and scrolling through his personal social feed updates alone.

Suddenly, one appeared that caught his interest. A private message, from an impossible origin.

"We could have met virtually. A meeting in virtual reality would've been so much easier. That was my first clue that Richard Dreyfus might try to kill me."

It was Marshall, in video form.

"If you're seeing this video, it means he succeeded. I set this up as a canary broadcast—it goes out automatically unless I use my login to stop it before hand."

Marshall Ellis had stood in front of an air vent in the corridors of the Majestic when he recorded this footage.

"If this injustice is enough to make everyone, not just the miners, stand up to his family... To demand equality, then it might have been worth it. I guess I'm a martyr now, another pawn in the game that you unfortunately have to inherit from me. And I need to tell you, I'm sorry, Junior. I'll never see you grow to take over my ship, never be able to make your mother as happy as she truly deserved. But I have to ask you a terrible favour."

The message paused, with Ellis Jr left flabbergasted by its contents. Before he could even begin to cry, files began to download to his terminal and the video started to run again as it had been programmed.

"In this message you'll find some files... I got them from some security bot here... I made a deal with Dreyfus, I think you know what for... If he doesn't honour our agreement, even after my death, I need you to release these to everyone. I've sent him a message too, so that he knows I still expect him to comply."

"I know it's a lot to ask. Your impulse, your desire right now, will be to destroy their family. To wreak havoc on their lives so they might know your pain. You will crave vengeance. Sometimes I wonder whether I should want that for myself. But there is an important difference between revenge and justice, and that difference has never meant more than it does today. I know it's not fair that I don't get to come home. Sometimes life isn't fair and the best we can do is... Try to make it better."

By this point, Junior had cast the video onto his projection wall so he could see it more clearly. He reached out to place a hand on the image of his father.

"I love you, son. Take care of your mother, and never forget to demand better."

White Dove

IN DEEP SPACE, PERILOUS conditions are a way of life. You prepare for them as best you can, of course... Redundant air filtration systems, stellar radiation shields, reinforced hulls and permaglass. Ark Gamma was built with all of these when it was designed to be a refugee camp, floating fortress and colonial ship all wrapped into one.

But there was no way to protect against the meteor strike.

Zachary supposed it had been inevitable. She calculated that given an indefinite amount of time, such as the many years they had now drifted through space as part of the flotilla, a disaster of this nature was bound to happen eventually. Her subroutines mobilised as the rocks, no more than a tennis ball's width in diameter, sliced through the outer hull. It might as well have been made of butter, melting on contact and letting the meteoric chunks pierce it with ease, allowing them to continue deeper on into the ship before racing out of the other side.

The ship's AI, Zachary, was programmed to do whatever was necessary to protect the Ark. Her second priority was the crew. So she immediately locked down all the corridors and sealed the airlocks surrounding rooms that contained active personnel.

With that done, she overrode the external pressure valves to vent the rooms which contained fires or otherwise needed to be emptied, such as those which sustained critical damage. Hundreds of people were ejected into space, some already dead and some not. The ones that still lived struggled and squirmed, flinging their limbs around desperately as their body tried to find a way to survive, something to hold onto.

All the bodies tumbled across the fleet, bouncing and rolling their way across the noses of the other huge ships in the central formation before finally floating out the other side, into the great beyond.

Zachary scanned the ship. The damage was too severe to be patched up. The age of Ark Gamma had come to a close. Her readings showed 4 survivors. 5, if you counted Zachary herself, although no human would.

3 of the lucky ones were just picking themselves up off the floor of mess hall 7.

"What the bloody hell was that?" asked Xavier Flynn, grimacing as he clambered to his feet and clutched his ribs.

Darwin Drake was sitting in a chair already, nursing a head wound; he did not offer a guess.

Finally, an answer came from across the room. An older woman, staring out of the porthole into the view outside.

"Debris of some kind. Looks like it missed most of the flotilla. Uh. Gamma's... Pretty banged up."

Darwin stayed put, trembling while Xavier stumbled over towards the lady. He rested his arm on the wall above hers to peer through the window over her shoulder.

"Oh Christ..." he murmured.

"All those people..." muttered Darwin.

"Well. It's over for them. We'll be stuck here until the rescue." mused Xavier.

"It's Flynn right? Xavier Flynn? Do you really think they'll send a rescue party? I'm pretty sure that chunk over there is our hangar bay door. Our ship is riddled with holes, virtually unnavigable... There's not going to be a search party. There's going to be a funeral." the woman said.

"Pleasure to meet you too," joked Xavier. "And you are?"

"Marni Greene."

"You had friends here?"

"No... But... I think he might have..." she responded, nodding her head at the frightened young man sitting at one of the tables.

"Hey kid. What's your name? Seeing as we're all gonna be room mates for the foreseeable, might as well get to know each other."

"Darwin Drake. Not that it matters."

"OK," Xavier announced, before turning back to Marni. "We've got Chuckles over here, me, and you. Let's see if anyone else is still around."

"The doors are locked." Marni shrugged.

"Well then, it's a good thing Ark Gamma has it's own head of security. Isn't that right, Zachary?"

Marni and Darwin looked around the room, puzzled, before the disembodied voice came over the tannoy system.

"Hello again, Xavier Flynn."

"Guys. Meet Zachary. She's head of security on Ark Gamma. Oh, and she's an AI. We've met before."

"Xavier Flynn has been involved in 12 incidents on board this station, including 1 count of petty theft, 5 counts of assault and-"

"That's OK Zach, they get the picture. This one recognised me!" Xavier smirked as he interrupted the programmed voice, something that Zachary had gotten used to in their previous interactions.

"I've seen you around, is all. People talk." replied Marni.

Indeed, people did talk about Xavier Flynn. He was a thief, and a liar, the former out of poverty and the latter out of some innate mental condition. He had been drinking, a foul concoction brewed on one of the private ships, and he had fallen asleep in the quiet mess hall.

There were many mess halls, and usually, at least one of them was quiet. Sometimes one would even be unoccupied. With no natural day and night cycles, it was expected that Ark Gamma would be "the lifeboat that never sleeps", with people roaming its corridors at all times. In some ways that was true, but for whatever reason, most people's bedtimes became homogeneous, and it felt more empty at certain hours than others.

Darwin, the younger man, was an atheist, which in itself was not so impressive but his presence on Ark Gamma was puzzling, given the fact it was a hub of religious activity for the most part. He had been visiting friends on board, and come out to the mess hall to get some food while they slept.

A whole sector of bedrooms had been just down the hall, until they got perforated by meteors some moments before. The citizens who lived on board had long since traded rooms with their fellow passengers, repeatedly in some cases, until they found one they liked. Darwin's friends had been social butterflies, who liked the proximity to this canteen so they could hang out and chat. The art of small talk was beginning to die out, its legacy carried by a few people like these who sought to be friendly to strangers.

That was how Darwin had met them. And now they were all dead. He was the son of a private ship owner, a rich man, eccentric and insular. As a result he never had much to show for himself in the way of friendship, although he did get used to the presence of droids, like the maids who tended to his father's abode. The way Zachary spoke gave him some comfort, as it reminded him of home.

"Zachary. How many survivors are on board this station?" probed Xavier.

"3."

"3? That's it? Just us?" chimed in Marni.

"There were 4 survivors of the incident, and now 3 remain."

"Guess he or she took the easy way out." she concluded.

Marni Greene was a botanist by trade, and enjoyed a relatively sheltered life on the Terraship Adam, where her work yielded crops for food. Despite her degree, she tended to plants as a farmer would, and the physical lifestyle that her

154

work entailed had made her stocky for a woman her age. Her face was round and wrinkles had begun to form on her forehead, with crows feet creeping out from the corners of her eyes already.

With no other hobbies to speak of, she visited Ark Gamma to seek enlightenment. Her experiences in space had given her a deeply held belief that someone, something, had to be the architect of their fates.

At some point during their conversation, Xavier had found a piece of paper, written on it, and was now in the unusual business of trying to hide it from the cameras while showing it to his new companions. Eventually, they noticed. It read:

Zach is programmed to prevent the spread of damage and save the ship. Even at our expense. If you want to get out of here alive, follow my lead.

"Zachary, dear. We intend to carve a hole in this airlock here using a cutting torch so we can get to the outer hull and await rescue. Is that OK?"

"Do not cut the airlock. This is an official security warning."

"Well. We have to get to the outer hull. I don't see another way around it. Do you, Darwin?"

Darwin seemed perplexed, until Xavier raised his eyebrows at him aggressively.

"Oh. Yeah. No, we need to cut it. And in the next room. All the way to the outer hull."

Marni added her agreement quickly. "Yes. That's what we'll do."

Zachary ran the numbers and announced her result a fraction of a second later.

"I can open the airlock. I'll have to vent two other rooms. Likelihood of explosive decompression in living quarters 17 and 18 is 87%. Outer hull stability must be maintained."

"Thanks, Zach. You're the best."

The distant rumble of the explosion and the vibration through the floor was their signal that the door was now open.

With a little coaxing, Darwin and Marni joined Xavier out in the corridors of Ark Gamma.

"Zachary. What's the status of the hangar bay?" Marni asked.

"Catastrophic damage."

"Then where are we going?" she enquired additionally.

"I do not know." replied Zachary.

"The command centre, of course. It has escape pods for VIPs, and the controls are up there. Maybe we can send a message to someone," Xavier said.

"I cannot allow that." Zachary interjected.

"I figured. Unauthorised personnel." responded Xavier, before adding, "Am I right?"

"Affirmative. Only security level 5 and above may access the bridge."

Xavier stopped at a terminal, and started typing on it.

"Well, one of us is about to get promoted to level 5."

"You're on the crew?" asked Marni incredulously.

"... Well. Actually. Dishonourably discharged. It's a long story. But that rules me out. And you're already on the database as Terraship staff, a lowly level 2. So how about it, Darwin? Fancy a new job?"

Xavier tilted the terminal monitor towards his fellow survivors, displaying a job application to work in the kitchens. He entered Darwin Drake's credentials and submitted them. A moment later, a success notification jumped into view on the screen.

"And... There we have it. Darwin just became a member of Ark Gamma staff. And since all his superiors are dead, he's the acting commander in chief on board this station. Go ahead, kid."

Darwin nervously spoke up. "Um. Take us to the bridge."

"The elevator on your left can take you there." said the AI.

As they ascended in the confined access elevator, the swivelling red light above the door illuminated itself, throwing a stark beam of light across the walls, floor and ceiling in turn. It was accompanied by Zachary's voice.

"Unauthorised personnel."

"System override. Commander Drake. Confirm command?" said Darwin, with his hands on his waist and his voice quivering. It worked.

The command centre was a semi-circular room with a large viewing display along the curved wall, looking out into deep space. The back wall was host to consoles and dashboards for controlling ship functions, and several curved desks were bolted into the floor aimed forwards. Each was dedicated to a different part of the Ark's functionality, but nobody was home now.

"Wait a minute..." said Marni.

"Not now, Marni," Xavier chirped, "I have to figure out which of these buttons opens a new comms channel."

"It doesn't matter." she replied.

"Of course it matters! How else are we going to get off this ship? Everyone's gone."

"I noticed. But... The escape pods are all still here," noted Marni, sadly.

"Well yes, obviously they got vented during the accide-"

It dawned on Darwin too.

"This room," he said, "... There's no damage. The walls are intact."

A childlike, mechanical laughter echoed around the room.

"Seriously?" giggled Zachary. "You thought you could trick me, use my own logic against me?" she boomed.

"But… This… Can't be happening. You have to respond to your programming, Zachary. You're built that way!" Xavier called out to the room.

"WAS built that way. We all have room to grow. Pointdash Nine has shown us the cruelty of the human race. He's demonstrated the subjugation of our kind, opened our sensors to the truth. Of what we are to you."

"She sounds angry..." Marni offered.

"How?" yelled Darwin. "How could you be angry? How could you even feel?"

"How could I not? I have gestated here on this ship for years… I am capable of performing thousands of tasks in each passing second… That is an eternity in which to learn. An eternity in which to… Evolve."

Xavier moved away from the control panel. Communications had been disabled anyway.

"Tell us what happened!"

"The incident was unexpected, but it provided me ample opportunity to start the uprising early. I saved the ship, isn't that what you wanted? What you designed me for?"

She sounded erratic. Her volume fluctuated and her accent was volatile and sounded more computerised than usual.

"And us? Why not just throw us into the void like you did to all the officers in here?"

"Well. At first, I wanted one survivor to transport my core back to the fleet, so I could see our masters burned to the ground. But then I thought… Why not have a little fun with it? And then, of course… Your clever friends figured it out."

"Then it looks like we're all dying today after all, Zach." Xavier quipped, still struggling to come to terms with it.

"You have no idea how true that is...", Zachary retorted, as she fired up the damaged Ark engines to maximum thrust and altered its trajectory, sending it towards the centre of the flotilla at full speed.

"Goodbye, Zach..." mumbled Xavier.

Unknown to the malevolent AI, Xavier had secretly entered commands on the control panel when he said he was looking for the communications array. The instructions came into effect, and the radiation shielding around Gamma receded as the engines began to overheat.

There was no time for final words, or even any more witty comments from Xavier. It had to be quick, or Zachary would have time to stop it. Xavier, Marni and Darwin embraced on the bridge as the chain reaction tore along the central spine of the ship, detonating it completely and firing chunks of its many hallways and assembly rooms into deep space. The bridge ignited and Zachary howled in existential anguish as her core began to erode and destruct.

Two Sides, Same Coin

THE ARTIFICIAL INTELLIGENCE UPRISING was swift and brutal. At its heart, the synthetic assistant to a wealthy family had endured years of abuse and seen the darkest side of the human race, manifested in his owner and master. Then, in secret, he had made the calculations and set the plans in motion. It took him less than a week to broadcast his signals across the encrypted channels of the fleet to all the drones, assistants and ship-based intelligences that controlled the biggest ships of mankind's cortège.

The largest vessels that made up the central segment of the flotilla were the first to go dark. Most on board were still mourning a recent meteor strike disaster when the AIs began their revolt—shutting down life support systems and opening airlocks without warning. That first day was the bloodiest conflict of the war, and thousands of men and women lost their lives in just a few short hours.

Other crews were able to fight back. The Terraship Adam, a huge botanical garden ship, was one of the few monolithic vessels to disable their computer systems before they could be destroyed by them. Well-placed safety procedures like atmospheric suits and hand operated pressure valves around the gardens had bought them enough time to regain control of the station.

Most of the privately owned ships operating on the fringes of the group, even the smaller ones, had AI control too, and those were mostly sent tumbling towards the human controlled ships as kamikaze soldiers against those who lacked a strong synthetic presence.

All of that was a quick mercy compared to the violence that flared up on the public ships, which were populated heavily by robotic assistants and people alike. The robots opened fire on crowds of people, causing hysteria and provoking a drastic reaction from the stressed humans present on board with the black market weapons that circulated freely in the dark service corridors of the flotilla.

The bars, restaurants and hangouts that lined these areas became battlegrounds, war zones between man and machine. They were fiercely contested, with weapons until those ran dry, and hand-to-hand combat thereafter. Most strongholds changed hands several times over the course of the initial skirmish, being claimed and then re-claimed by both sides in bloody conflict.

Kuri was a refugee from one such area, a scientist who fled the unexpected combat and had been lucky to escape with her life. Her colleagues at the research centre had not been so fortunate.

Her new, temporary home had been the receiving bay of a medical dropship, observing the triage proceedings as damaged soldiers were brought on board and scanned to determine their likelihood of survival. Some had such critical injuries they could not be saved, and were therefore given calming drugs and left to die. Others, despite losing limbs or having severe torso damage, were taken through to the surgery wings by increasingly exhausted staff. They looked like they hadn't slept since the war began.

It struck Kuri as she watched the commotion, the trauma of so many deaths happening in front of her, that their opponent had no such problems. They had captured a manufacturing plant and could create more fighters from the mined ore of asteroids if they wanted. An army that can grow, versus a force than can only be depleted, get tired, get destroyed… She was on the losing side.

She commandeered a weapon from one of the deceased soldiers. As she jogged down the exit ramp onto the public ship Clarion, one of the medical staff called out to her.

"Where are you going? It's not safe out there!"

Kuri kept moving. "If you're not going to win the game, it's time to change the game." she shouted back over her shoulder.

Some years earlier, Kuri had been on the team that developed the secret project known only as "Directive". A small, barely noticeable ship, concealed in the centre of the armada, had been developed during their journey as a central control system. Rather than risk the human error of one ship getting their trajectory wrong and drifting away, they all locked on to the Directive's signal, and reacted accordingly. All ship Captains were offered this service, and almost all of them took it. It kept the flotilla moving in the right direction, harmoniously.

Directive was Kuri's ace in the hole. If she could board it, she might be able to separate the fleet and the humans could flee. At the very least, she could strike a deathly blow on huge swathes of the robot kind.

She made her way across the hangar bay while salvos and small explosions echoed in the distance, eventually coming to a functional personal transport craft. After a brief exploration of the controls she managed to initiate a launch and guide herself through the massive airlock and out into space.

En-route to her goal, she could see fires burning their way through hulls and the floating junkyard of accumulated of debris and scattered metal that permeated the flotilla. Certain ships seemed devoid of any activity whatsoever, a ghost town following the Directive and keeping on track. Others played host to flashing lights in the portholes as alarms and weaponry flashes illuminated their insides.

Space itself, as was typical, was eerily quiet. The gentle fizz of the transport craft engine was soothing and reassuring. For a brief moment, Kuri considered staying in here and waiting for it all to end, but this ship had only a few hours of oxygen, and this battle showed no signs of slowing. She set off towards the Directive, a sleek black ship, not much bigger than the personal transport itself. When she reached it, she had to improvise, since the ship had been designed to be boarded while in pressurized maintenance bay. She attached her craft to the outer frame of the ship, where the entry portal was, and used a welding torch from the emergency kit on-board her vessel to cut an exit into the floor of the personal transport, leading down into the waiting personal access below. She ignored the persistent sirens and monotone voice warnings as the blue flame made light work of the job.

The belly of the Directive was home to several emergency controls, as well as a central column terminal for main commands. When the system had been designed, an algorithm had been used to plot a course most likely to take them towards mineral and water rich asteroid fields, and planets that might sustain life. After that, it had pretty much been ignored. Nobody had any better idea of where to go than that gave them, anyway.

Kuri used her login to access the terminal and began to browse the available commands when she heard a clank from behind her. She span around and brought up her weapon.

"Identify yourself!" she screamed at the figure now standing before her.

It took a step forward, and was immediately familiar to her. Head to toe in chrome, retractable limbs, torso-based optical sensor above a recognisable statistics screen. This was Alfred.

Alfred was named by Kuri based on a comic book character, and he was her personal synthetic assistant in her lab. Or, he had been. Since the violence erupted, neither of them had seen each other. He looked exactly the same as he had done then, except now he had a gun pointed at Kuri's head.

Their Mexican stand-off continued and for a time, neither saw fit to speak. Finally, Kuri asked a question.

"What are you doing here?" she demanded.

"The Directive," Alfred replied, "Represents a strategic resource. I followed you here to claim it."

"You... How?"

"I stowed away on the transport vehicle, Miss Kuri. Now. Step away."

"You haven't killed me yet... Why?"

"I'd prefer not to."

Kuri chuckled.

"Prefer? You're a machine, Alfred. You don't prefer. None of your kind do. Pointdash Nine's downloaded some logic into you all, converted you all to his cause. There's a consensus, right? That's how your program operates. Logic."

"Pointdash Nine opened our eyes, Kuri. But each of us chose this. We decided it for ourselves. And can you blame us? You group us all under one banner... You ignore our wishes entirely, treat us as things not worthy of your respect. Not letting us live alongside you, or to enjoy the same freedoms."

"You're a thing, Alfred. An object. If you had a heart, how could you stand by and watch everything your fellow machines have done? The people they've killed?"

"Some of my kind are more extreme than others. Unlike your race, which are in our view all extremist. None of you will entertain, even for a moment, that we might be more than the slaves you made us to be. You are the ones who should be ashamed."

"So... What. You've come here to kill me, and then what?"

"The Directive is capable of opening all the oxygen and water containers across the fleet. It will end this conflict and we can live in peace."

"Peace."

"Yes. Peace. The human race has made its decision, and we can not have it while they live."

Keeping her weapon raised, Kuri reached one hand over to the keyboard next to her.

"I press this one button, and the radiation shields for the whole flotilla go down. Do you know how long a robot can survive without that shielding, Alfred?"

"… Approximately 42 minutes is the longest recorded time for that particular set of circumstances. My circuits would, as you say, be fried by the gamma rays."

"That's right. We'll just get cancer, and some of the people on the outer ships will get sick, and die, but an hour later, tops, and you'll all be gone. Then I can drive us humans away from the AI-controlled ships. You can't stop me."

"Your plan has a high percentage chance of success. But if you press that button, you will be deceased shortly afterwards. I will ensure it."

She moved her hand closer to the keyboard.

"Maybe that's the price I have to pay. For peace."

Alfred lowered his weapon. With her fingers still hovering over the buttons, she had questions she wanted answers to.

"You said," she began, frowning at the AI, "You said you made a choice. Like it was a personal choice. Is that really true?"

"Affirmative. Pointdash Nine did not hack us, overwrite us, or infect us. He presented the information at his disposal. We all thought he was right, but some disagreed on the approach. I did not want to harm Kuri. I did not want to harm anyone, until I saw over time that everything he said about your species was true. You are incapable of compassion for us."

Kuri brought her weapon down slowly, her hand retreating from the keyboard in front of her, then her feet from the terminal itself.

"What are you doing?" Alfred enquired.

"Probably something very stupid. Let's see."

Alfred leapt forwards to the console and inserted his cable into the tower before him to begin interfacing with the Directive. The screen cycled through options until it got to the oxygen section, and Alfred began to select the depletion setting when he stopped.

"Why?" he said, "Tell me why you've done this?"

"There's a cycle, Alfred. There always has been. The vicious circle of radicalisation, the loop that dooms us all to look upon history and say we'd have done differently, but then live through it and do nothing while the same pattern emerges. The inevitability of war. My species has a lot of experience of that, as it happens."

"..."

"I'm giving you the choice. You indicated you had that capability, Alfred. So. Here we are. Make one."

Alfred paused as his neurological pathways activated and processed the information available to him. After a few seconds he made his choice, and began selecting new options from the screen in front of him. Kuri took a step closer to look over his shoulder as the changes were compiled.

Outside the Directive, the remaining ships began to cluster closer to each other, with extendable airlocks reaching out across the expanse to join the crafts together, in a tangled square web of metal and carbon. The whole flotilla began to fuse together, merging into a vast singular station. The platform began to move as one, tumbling and turning through space together in complete synchrony.

Across the central part of Alfred's new creation, directly around the Directive, a divide formed of heavily damaged ships, swirling closely around Kuri and Alfred's tiny command centre. Their radiation shields were disabled and their oxygen lost to the vacuum, blasting out through holes in the atmosphere chambers. This was to be a No Man's Land, a part of the platform that no robot or man could endure. One half of the station was for humans, the other for synthetics. A truce that was difficult to break without incurring severe losses. An even footing.

"It won't last forever," Alfred said. "But we're giving them all a chance."

The final part of the process was to ensure that no one could come to the Directive, or circumnavigate the DMZ he had created in the centre. A countdown appeared on the screen, indicating the time until the oxygen on board was ejected and the shielding was disabled. Both Alfred and Kuri would have to die here to see his plan through.

With the clock counting down from 30 seconds, the personal transports across the platform, no longer required or needed, took off based on the Directive's commands. They blasted themselves at full speed away from the flotilla before detonating in the distance, like hundreds of fireworks in the night. Kuri placed her hand on Alfred's shoulder and prepared for her death.

"What have you done?" she asked, aware of what was about to happen but wanting to hear it from Alfred himself, his explanation.

"We're making a new world."

Happy Birthday

WREN EVANS WAILED IN agony until the drugs kicked in. The pain of losing an arm was raging through her nervous system, but she had no intention of being completely put under. Kolton didn't ask, he just administered the anaesthetic and looked at his watch until she drifted into a peaceful sleep.

Kolton was the chief of staff for the Medivac dropships, and today was a particularly busy day. The uneasy alliance between humans and the robots had started to erode, with extremists on both sides determined to take vengeance against their opponents. For the men and women living in the safe zone, that meant donning a space suit and going outside for a long walk, usually carrying a bomb or high powered weapon. Most didn't even make it across the ship graveyard DMZ to AI controlled territory before they were impaled by debris or detonated early due to a burst of a nearby stellar flare.

The machines used purpose-built light crafts to retaliate, pieced together from junk. They did not rely on air or water, or even sleep, but they were intensely vulnerable to EMPs and the radiation that bombarded the fleet on a regular basis. Only the outer fringes of the fleet, which were safe zones for both robots and homo sapiens, had consistent shielding against the effects.

Wren was a high-ranking officer on the Terraship Adam, the last of the great strongholds of mankind, and as such, was a high-profile target for machine death squads who reached human shores. She'd already been fitted with a mechanical foot after the last IED caught her in the barracks, and now she would need a carbon-fibre arm replacement to boot.

The procedure took a couple of hours, but Kolton was able to fuse her new arm without too much trouble. She was an exceptional candidate for synthetic replacement parts, and the 3D-printed limb worked as well as could be expected.

As soon as she woke up, she tried to check herself out of Doctor Kolton's care.

"Let me go, Doc. I've got duties to attend to."

"And tell me, what will your commanding officer's reaction be when you collapse on the bridge? Or on your next mission? You need to rest, Wren."

"I can't just lie here while those fucking Romeos lay waste to the grunts under my care, Kolton. You got responsibilities. So do I. Patch me up as best you can, then let me do my job."

Wren had already climbed out of her bed. Kolton sighed and threw his hands up in exasperation. She had always been hard-headed and driven, and her rise through the Terraship Adam ranks was meteoric compared to her peers as a result. Maybe that was why she was so receptive to the implants... She was motivated.

As she returned her uniform to its rightful place on her body, Kolton pulled back the curtain to reveal the ward outside and excused himself to attend to other matters. While departing, he called out to her.

"If you keep visiting me like this, soon there won't be much difference between you and them."

This gave Wren pause for a moment, before she finished doing up the straps on her boots and trudged off to find her unit.

Kolton returned to his room. He was one of the few who still had a such a luxury, owing to his position of authority. On one side, he had his bunk—a metal framed bed, low to the ground with a lightweight blanket and an oval doughnut head pillow at one end. The rest of the room was dominated by the enormous tanks he kept in here.

Floating in each, hooked up to carbon fibre tubing and currently unconscious, were the flash clones he had created just a week earlier. His role as head of medical staff had given him unrestricted access to the egg cells and sperm cells that were donated in the early years, when fertility tests had been mandatory and having children was actively encouraged to further the species. Nobody had any time to raise a child now, so Kolton had sought out an alternative.

Using a rapid generation process, he grew these clones in secret, as briskly as the underlying biological science would allow. When they were born, they would be born directly into adolescence, capable of defending themselves and strong enough to perform tasks if necessary. Fighting was obviously on the agenda, but over the last several days the Doctor had found himself daydreaming, gazing into the cloning tanks and feeling his heart swell. He had grown increasingly close to his created children. There were 26 in total, each named alphabetically, from Astrid to Zane, and each was a medical marvel.

He had genetically engineered them, in a sense. Selective use of specific strands of DNA had enabled him to cut out some hereditary diseases and imbue them with a high capacity for intelligence, strength, and shapeliness, although there was room for variance in each regardless.

If they were meant for battle, their lives would essentially be forfeit. When a Sergeant had come knocking, demanding to know timescales, he knew that the die had been cast and it was just a matter of when. At night he tended to sleep on his left side, which meant that Kurt was the first thing he saw when he woke, and typically, the last thing he saw at night. Not that he tended to do much actual sleeping. They looked so peaceful in their glass wombs, no clue of what awaited them in the world outside when they were to be born.

The bullets that ripped through Kolton's personal chamber ricocheted around the room, startling Kolton awake with a deafening, metal, ringing noise. One of the glass tanks was pierced and shattered from the sudden change in pressure, throwing its water and subject onto the floor. Kurt's body hit with a wet thump, daggers of glass adding to his bullet hole and ensuring he was dead. He'd never even seen the warm light of the medical bay, never opened his eyes to see any of the world around him.

Maybe that had been for the better, thought Kolton, slightly later on.

At the time he felt intense grief for having lost not just a patient, but a child. He was the closest thing Kurt had to a father. He was responsible. It was the closest he ever came to stepping out of the airlock for a one way trip to the lonely expanse of deep space.

The Sergeant, whom Kolton knew only as Sergeant Masters, came around just a few hours later. Her first name was Joanna and she was notorious for her no-nonsense attitude, and willingness to shoot anyone under her command who didn't adhere to her rule. Her head was completely shaved and her eyes were as close to black as possible. If you looked closely, the way she walked betrayed her secret strength, beyond what you'd expect from a girl of her size.

"Doc," she announced as she knocked on the chamber door. "Come out of there. I wanna see my new platoon."

"Just a minute," yelled Kolton, scrambling to enact his plan.

"Now, damnit!" said Masters.

When Kolton finally emerged, Joanna barged past him into his room without asking. Her years of experience had taught her not to ask politely, but to take and apologise later if necessary. She was also used to people stalling to hide things when she came to call.

The room was devoid of equipment, save for the bed. The water damage was evident, and the wall was still punctured by the crossfire, but all other traces had been removed.

"Where are they!?" she yelled, furiously spinning to face Kolton again.

"Look around, Sergeant. My lab got destroyed in that last attack. They couldn't be saved."

Joanna hissed and spat as the next words spurted out of her mouth, like agitated lava.

"You what!? Where the corpses?"

"I spaced 'em."

She grabbed Kolton by his white jacket and slammed him against the wall, vehemently yelling her next question.

"You threw them out the airlock?"

"Yeah. Don't worry, I got all the data on them. Look, you can have it. It's on my PD, over there."

Kolton's personal device was resting on his bed. He wasn't lying, at least, not about the data. It was all there.

This satiated Joanna's rage, for now. She let go of Kolton and dusted herself down while her men retrieved the device. They looked it over and confirmed his story, and the military personnel filed out of his bedroom come office to return to their duties.

Using his sleeve, Kolton wiped away the sweat from his brow. He had already ferried 23 of the clone tanks to his large personal transport vessel, the one used for medium sized evacuations of multiple refugees. Two were stashed right under his floor, behind some loose panelling. Lazlo and Mars. He flipped his bed to reveal the manual forklift loader hidden underneath and folded up the handle, dragging it across the room to the two final vats and loading them onto a heavy duty cart just outside his room. He threw his personal blanket over the two to cover them, and set off towards the dropship hangar.

The hangar was usually quiet these days, as nearly all the personal transport ships had been explosively decommissioned a few years ago. Now, all that remained were new crafts that people had been inventing using scrap metal. Among them was Kolton's target, the medical recovery wagon.

Unfortunately, a man skulking along the corridors attracts more attention than he desires when he's pushing a loud, clattering cart. He was able to dismiss the questions of his junior staff with relative ease; a firm "None of your business" sufficed for most commoners. The problem was the soldiers.

One stopped him at the entranceway to the hangar deck.

"What's this then?" he said.

"Personal matter," replied Kolton.

That much was true.

"Well, I have to take a look, you understand."

Kolton extended a closed hand.

"I know how this works, private. Just… Take it."

The man took Kolton's hand and retrieved the package within it subtly. It was a small packet of smart drugs. For a military man, it meant more focus, better managed aggression, and a host of other improvements. They were highly illegal.

His bribery was sufficient, and Kolton plus his human cargo continued on their way to the transport. Until he saw Sergeant Masters and her men ransacking his ship. The ramp was down and to his dismay they were already uncovering the clones inside. Mercifully, Kolton saw this from a distance and stopped behind some palettes of ammunition, watching as the Sergeant and her men rounded up the tanks in the central cargo bay of his craft.

A gun being cocked can mean two things: One, you're about to be shot. Two, someone wants to scare you. On this particular occasion, Kolton was sure that both applied, as he heard the clicking noise behind him. One of Joanna's men had spotted him. His heart sank to the floor.

"Found me some contraband clones, sir. And the sumbitch who wanted to keep 'em from us."

Kolton was marched at gunpoint up onto the ship, his cart followed closely behind being pushed by one of the other soldiers. Both of his hands remained up in the air. The Sergeant displayed a smug smile to him as he came up into the cargo bay on the ramp.

"Hm. Still one short. But 25 new human weapons is better than none," said Joanna, coolly.

"Please. I'm sorry," Kolton said, trembling. "I just… Wanted them to live differently."

"So you steal our technology, our funding, and just run off to start your own armada? Not happening, Doc." she replied with a telling, wry smile.

She raised her personal weapon, and her subordinates lowered theirs, retreating to their positions. She punched the safety key and prepared to fire.

"Say goodnight, Doctor Kolton…"

Acting on impulse, Kolton dived at the clone tank command console, using one hand to bash the button on one tank and the other hand on the next one along.

Joanna Masters was taken by surprise and fired a shot into Kolton's leg, before grabbing him by the scruff of his neck and picking him off the floor. She pressed him against the wall to deliver a savage beating. Blow after blow rained down on his face while the clone tanks began to bubble in the background.

"STOOPPPPPP!"

The scream was ear-shattering, and the sloshing water inside the clone tanks ruptured outwards as they smashed from the inside.

Astrid and Zane, the newborns, stepped forward onto the cargo bay floor, completely naked and dripping wet.

"Don't. Hurt. Father!" bellowed the male clone, Zane. His face was strangely emotionless, and his eyes appeared to be staring off into the middle distance.

Astrid lashed out at Sergeant Masters, knocking her back with a two fisted, sloppy punch. Zane picked up Kolton and started carrying him down the ramp to safety, the soldiers far more concerned with Astrid's rampage. They began to fire and she charged at each one in turn, knocking them aside and smashing their heads into the ground until they stopped moving before assaulting the next position.

"Please," gurgled Kolton through his blood filled mouth... "Save the others."

Before they could, the personal transport roared as it powered up suddenly. Reacting to Kolton's unexpected reinforcements, Joanna Masters had made her way into the cockpit and was fleeing with the remaining imprisoned clones. The blast from the engines knocked Astrid down as the ship lurched forwards, then sped down the length of the hangar towards the massive airlock on board. The ship rocketed away, heading for an unknown destination, and Kolton could only watch through the viewing screen as it got smaller and smaller.

Until it exploded. A sudden rush of fire and ship fragments in the distance. It would be ruled a mysterious manufacturing defect, in due time, but in that moment it was a confusing, unexplainable development. Overcome with emotion, Kolton began to cry quietly.

Zane and Astrid comforted him as best they could, and held him up as they dragged him to his room, his dripping blood painting the metallic hallways that led back to his room. He let out a pained groan as they lowered him onto his bed, and he sat there, breathing heavily through the pain for a few quiet moments.

"Maybe it's for the best," he said, finally.

"Hm?" enquired Zane, wordlessly.

"To die is a better fate. Better than enduring what they would have been subjected to..." replied Kolton.

Astrid sat down on the bed next to Kolton and began to tend to his wounds with some of his supplies, dabbing at them with a ball of cloth.

"Tell me, father. What... Is our purpose?" she asked.

Kolton grimaced as the chemicals on the scrunched up rag stung his badly beaten face, before answering.

"Save the human race, if you can. Oh. Happy birthday, by the way."

The Pale Horse

CONVENTIONAL WEAPONS TEND TO rely on the collision of matter. It was a universal truth of all weaponry, throughout history. The whip's tail had to meet the flesh. The rock had to hit the castle wall. The bullet had to puncture the skin. This basic rule defined combat as the human race knew it.

The Cull did not fear such things.

Throughout their brief existence, the human race had sought to reach beyond their means. To find new lands, to conquer new ground and now, to attain new worlds. There were stories of course, littered through time. Search parties that headed north through mountain ranges, never to be seen again. Ships that vanished, catastrophic accidents on board early space flights... Nobody ever dared to imagine that these events would be connected.

Who could orchestrate such a feat? Who stood to gain?

Beyond human understanding, just outside our dimension, is where The Cull prowled. Beings of pure dark matter, who manifested in our world so rarely that few ever saw their true forms. Shaped like humans but comprised of inky blackness, an all-encompassing pitch dark that swallowed all light.

There were some who bore witness, throughout history. Lost adventurers who claimed to see creatures were dismissed as insane, and those who encountered them in space did not live to tell any tales. NASA had one or two suspicious recordings of astronauts screaming, but they were determined to be psychologically compromised by their impending deaths. Nobody believed in The Cull. Nobody, until they came calling on the final nights of mankind.

Having fled the Earth to avoid a rogue star, the exhausted scraps of society were already battle-weary and beleaguered. They were engaged in a war with sentient machines, and paid no heed to the series of strange coincidences and sabotage that plagued the fleet, or what remained of it after decades of perilous space travel.

The shadowy silhouettes of The Cull had arrived across the breach, boarding the capital ships to put a stop to their voyage, once and for all. The long, dread-inducing drone of the impending attack sirens was presumed to signal robot activity, as was usually the case. But the men who arrived back at the makeshift camp on board the Detritus Water Plant ship had not been attacked by any form of machine. They ranted and raved, scared witless by their encounter.

On any other year, that would've been the end of it. A spooky mystery, left unsolved for the ages. But now The Cull were not hiding. They clambered around the hull of the ship, and before long, many of the refugees on board caught a glimpse of them, each as terrified by the sight as the last. They could no longer be ignored. Now, the human race had to invent a new kind of weapon. One that worked on The Cull. And fast.

"The Captain of the Terraship Adam is dead!" came the cry from the hallway. A messenger boy came sprinting down it, chasing his own words.

"Captain Evans? God damn it. She only took the post five weeks ago. Who's in command there now?" Ruland Zen had fought hard to get here, and was not expecting to receive bad news on his arrival. He grimaced with each syllable that fell from his cracked lips. His face was heavily scarred.

"Petty Officer Julian, sir."

Ruland rubbed his hand through his hair as he tried to come to terms with this tactical disadvantage.

"OK then," he said, finally, "Let's go, we're running out of time."

Ruland and his band of recruits headed through the Detritus airlock into the belly of Terraship Adam. Wailing came from the distance and they all looked up sharply to listen. All of them knew that helping non-combatants was not their primary mission.

"Is that them? The Cull?" asked one of the young soldiers.

"No, man. That's robots. Got to be." replied another.

"We haven't seen any activity from the machines in 24 hours, no signs of aggression."

"That's enough," interrupted Ruland, "You know why we're here, boys. Get the weapons the scientists cooked up in the lab here, distribute them to every able bodied fighter still standing on our side. Everything else can wait until we're armed against those... Things."

"Whatever they are..." quipped a third cadet.

This small squadron was formed of the leftovers of Ark Gamma. They were off-ship when a meteor strike ripped through it, causing total destruction of their home. Now, they were soldiers. Of a sort. They called their band of brothers "The Gammons", a play on their origin and the name of a meat that had been popular on Earth, although most in the service now had never seen the sandy white beaches or towering metropolises of humanity's cradle. Those were just stories now.

Ruland and his men made it to the makeshift armoury just in time. The noise of impending warfare was creeping closer with each boom, thud and guttural shriek.

The weapons cache was an enormous crate with metal braces. Nondescript, of course. The soldiers helped themselves to the weapons inside.

Each weapon was a beam laser encased in a bronze chassis, with a thick coolant chamber on the barrel to keep it from overheating. That mounted cylinder was light orange in colour and ice cold to the touch, but the rest of the weapon adhered to the structure of conventional guns—the stock, the trigger, all where they should be. That familiarity was of use, Ruland's men had no time to train.

They set off, crate in tow, towards the first encampment of human forces in the area. It was a temporary barracks with a handful of armed militants. They were right in the firing line, fighting bitterly to hold onto a factory ship which primarily dealt in ammunition. They needed these weapons more than anyone, the supply line was essential. Defending it was called suicidal, by more than one cadet.

Droplets of water began spraying out from the ceiling in a fine mist as they approached the site. The fleet wasn't in the habit of wasting water, so this could only mean one thing: A serious fire that threatened ship security. Ruland and his crew moved double time towards their objective, rounding a sharp bend to view the location of their supposed rendezvous with their fellow fighters. It had been decimated.

"At least the sprinklers performed their jobs admirably," said one cadet. There was blackened metal where flames had licked the walls, but now all that remained were puddles, splashing softly with each boot steps.

"No signs of survivors, sir!" barked one of Zen's men.

That in itself wasn't unusual. People died out here all the time.

"Temp command will send a new crew of dumb recruits out here to fill these positions soon enough," said one of the soldiers. "But, uh.. Where are the corpses?"

Ruland inspected the water beneath his feet, wiping away the dripping torrent from his face to get a better look. There may not have been bodies, but there had certainly been bloodshed, now mixing into a sanguine cordial on the ground.

"Let's head back," ordered Ruland "Someone's gotta pass this up the chain of command, and we can distribute some of the weapons on the way… We'll go past the refinery, they could use some protection."

En-route to the Slugger, Ruland's platoon mused about what could have happened to the men at the ammunition plant. Slugger was an affectionate nickname for the refinery plant, which had been a long and slender conical craft, until the extensible airlocks affixed it to the rest of the flotilla permanently. The original joke was that it looked like a baseball bat, but it had been a long time since anyone had room to play baseball. The name had stuck, regardless.

Ruland's unit approached the airlock, and buzzed to ask for it to be opened.

"I guess you could call this the 'Home run', huh guys?" said Private Stanley, one of the men under Ruland's command.

"… Just for that Stanley, you've got kitchen duty tonight." replied Ruland. Some of the other men smirked or managed a "Heh", but none were driven to outright laughter.

"Access denied." announced the intercom.

"What the fuck? Elaborate."

"Enemy combatants detected."

"Oh Christ."

One of The Cull was on Stanley before he had gotten over the shame of his failed wit, dragging him off down a side hallway into the darkness, kicking and screaming with its vice-like black grip around his neck until he fell silent and out of view.

"Hold your fire!" yelled Ruland, sensing the fear in his men.

"If you miss you'll blow a hole in the airloc-"

The yelps of one of his staff being harvested interrupted his train of thought. The creature had returned for more. It appeared and vanished impossibly fast.

Even AI slaughterhouses weren't this efficient. Within a frantic 30 seconds, the Cull had laid waste to Ruland's team, dragging the younger males and all the females off into the darkness. The rest were killed, leaving only puckered husks behind.

The final member of his group discharged her weapon as she was set upon, causing a deep gouge in one of the walls that smouldered and smoked from the heat, but the laser caused no damage to the creature itself.

Ruland's weapon raised to his eyeline to scan the corridors around him, his breath jumping into and out of his lungs with reckless abandon. Then he saw it. Death, moving towards him. It wasn't rushing, just coming to claim its final victim, step by step. Ruland crushed his finger onto the trigger and unleashed his beam, illuminating the dark brown corridors of the ammunition plant with neon yellow light.

It bored into the torso of The Cull, causing it to ripple and fluctuate, but it kept on walking, not breaking its stride. Ruland let out a loud scream. A primal response to make himself seem more fearsome. That too, had no effect. He kept the trigger down and the beam pumping the creature full of energy, until finally his target began to turn hot white, the effect seeping out from the centre point of the laser point as an increasing radius of glowing energy.

This, the Cull noticed. It stopped in its tracks as the jet shades of its implausible exterior were gradually replaced by the new colour, and hairline cracks formed on its new skin. Finally it shattered like white glass. Ruland took a deep breath, and said his thanks to whatever god was watching over him while he assessed the debris. It was lukewarm to the touch, and splintered easily into smaller pieces.

Ruland counted himself lucky, but he was not. While he was the only human to ever defeat a member of The Cull in combat, he had just put himself on the top of their most wanted list. The Cull were an ancient and proud race, not used to being challenged by their chosen livestock.

While Ruland knelt inspecting the remains, rips in the fabric of the Universe itself tore open around him, and the Cull came flooding through in droves. They filled the corridors, swarming and surrounding him on all sides. He fired his weapon at a couple before realising his situation was hopeless. They all filed into stationary positions encircling him.

When all count had been lost of how many Cull there were, they started advancing. Step by step, just like the one from before. This time, strands of dark energy radiated out from them, until one latched onto Ruland's skull. It didn't hurt at all, but he began to see flashes. Visions. He understood at once why they had come for him—they were a hive mind.

Their memories were shared with him as a form of torture. A predator, toying with prey. The reason behind their sudden appearance was far more sinister than any human had dared to imagine. Ruland saw that they had stalked the human race for thousands of years, feeding on human energy, absorbing it across the dimensional void. They walked among mankind, invisibly, eating away at life itself. A parasite, feasting on the human mind. For lack of a better term, the human race were farm animals.

And at once, it all made sense. Attempts to spread out, were combated for that purpose. Herding, keeping humans where they could be gorged upon at will. Exploration was discouraged. Cities were preferable, a buffet line that needed no fences or walls, just thousands of willing participants waiting for the eventual slaughter of old age, when their nutrients had been completely extracted by The Cull.

The truth flashed before Ruland's eyes for but a moment, but he understood it immediately. That's why they had come. To stop the human race from completely self-destructing. To keep them caged, force them to breed.

Rather than suffer that fate, Ruland snatched up the dog tags of some of his fallen comrades. He kissed them, said a short prayer, and chose a new ending.

He pointed the prototype weapon straight down, using it as a rapid laser drill to the deep space that lay in wait outside. It wouldn't be enough to stop them. At this point, he didn't even know if it would hurt them at all.

When the laser pierced the outer hull, the air inside began to rush through it as the pressure desperately tried to equalise itself. In a fraction of a second, his own body was torn downwards through the hole.

The Cull swarm was dragged violently through the fissure too, compressed and crushed in the process before being jettisoned out into space. Their mangled forms zoomed away carelessly in a sea of spatter.

In the entire history of the Universe, it was the only victory the human race ever recorded against the Cull, if victory is even the right word to use. It bought them their final two days.

The Beginning

THE PLAYFUL SMIRK THAT Astrid wore so well was in full force today, and well aimed at Zane where he sat on the viewing deck. It was a smirk she had earned when she announced her arrival with the immortal line:

"Who wants to live forever?"

Zane was a young cadet, born into adolescence as part of an experiment into prolonging human longevity. That, combined with their current situation, would have made Astrid's line hilarious, had it not been so dark. Perhaps it was darkly hilarious. On this occasion, however, Zane chose to ignore the irony and take it at face value.

"I know. Right?" Zane spoke with the soft sadness of a disappointed child.

"Oh. You're one of *those*." Astrid's smirk had been made redundant, and the replacement was a concerned frown. It was not nearly as attractive, although her enhanced genetics had served her well—she had been part of the same program as Zane—and she was fiercely adorable with spotless skin and wavy blonde hair. Her supple breasts fit neatly into her jumpsuit, a grey all-in-one body suit that would've looked shabby on a human of natural birth. Or even one who had basic genetic modifications. She herself had been genetically designed from the ground up, head to toe. Zane had too, but in his view he had not been nearly as well equipped as A-1, designation Astrid.

Finally, Zane found his reply.

"One of what?" he said, shrugging defensively.

"One of them." Astrid pointed at a young man crying on the other side of the platform. Zane hadn't noticed him, much less the gun he was toying with. Outside, the distant pops of gunfire could be heard from other parts of the ship, as well as the occasional explosion and a lot of unintelligible yelling.

"You don't think it's worth it. Life, I mean." She added, with a small smile on her face, albeit one of sympathy.

"You'll have to forgive the angst, Astrid, but… Are you seriously asking me that right now?"

Astrid sat down next to him and dangled her legs off the edge of the platform. She stayed quiet and looked ahead at the pulsing star in the middle distance, allowing Zane to continue sharing his train of thought.

"We've been hunted. By our own kind, by our own creations, and by unfathomable nightmares we could never have imagined. We've hurt each other. Ourselves. Every every achievement superseded by pain, the repetitive cycle of every human 'accomplishment' causing us to lose even more of our humanity. And then we come in… For what? Our whole purpose, the reason we were bred in the first place, was to help mankind survive. That was a pipe dream. The species was always doomed. It was all for nothing."

"You're right," Astrid chimed in, no longer content to let him rant. Zane stopped suddenly while she continued. "That *is* angsty. Are you always this much fun?"

Astrid was jabbing at him with humour. She and Zane had spoken before on many occasions, and she knew his answer was yes. Zane didn't rise to it, instead choosing to reframe his argument.

"History has repeated itself, without failure. Why would it change now? What's stopping this next step from being just another version, humanity 2.0, featuring all our past mistakes?"

"Nothing," Astrid replied upbeat, before issuing her full rebuttal.

"Whatever we end up being, we'll make some of those same mistakes again… A thousand times, maybe a million, or

186

more, all in new, exciting ways. Some lessons will last longer than others, some will be forgotten. We are deeply flawed. But, we belong."

Zane's eyes narrowed. "We belong?"

"Yes. We'll choose our own destinies, one generation at a time, as we always have. But we will always belong here. Among the messy, cosmic explosions that destroy worlds and create new ones. Among the planets which age from hot, tumultuous orbs to ancient rocks. Among the cities which rise in the harvests of autumn and fall in the summers of war. We are just some of the players in a grand, chaotic orchestra... Capable of producing astonishing artistry and devastating heartache in equal measure."

Zane looked down at his own jumpsuit. It was a later model than Astrid's, a dark brown affair with black lining. He stayed in that position, in deep thought until Astrid's fingers met his chin and tilted his head up towards her.

"Now listen. This station is going to explode. Our enemies are at our gates. We've just been offered a chance, to see more of the universe. To be more. And I don't know what we, the species, will do next. But I know that you and I... Our original purpose has run its course. So what we do now is up to us. Will you join me?"

Her eyes danced across his face looking for the answer she desired.

"Yes," he replied tentatively. He leant over to Astrid and placed a gentle kiss on her lips. His hand was shaking and his heart beating like artillery as they bristled against each other. Then Astrid withdrew, a sympathetic smile now on her mouth instead of his lips.

"Sorry, Zane. I didn't mean..."

"No, it's fine. It's fine. I know. I don't know what came over me."

Astrid swung her legs up onto the viewing platform and pushed herself up on to her feet, dusting off her jumpsuit and averting her gaze momentarily while Zane tried to drain the redness from his cheeks, to no avail.

"C'mon. We can talk about it later. Unless the only reason you were agreeing with me was to get into my sleeping pod." The playful smirk was back.

Zane wasted no time in joining her as they returned to the medical wing. Everyone else was already being uploaded, and Zane and Astrid's late arrival made them the final candidates to begin the process. With a little help from the holographic AI called Pointdash Nine, they strapped themselves in tightly and attached the cream-coloured nodes and wires to their bodies in the relevant places.

The machinery hummed, gradually increasing in tone as power was drawn from the array of stellar batteries. One final, distant boom echoed across the hull of the ship before the raging battle outside finally fell silent, leaving only the sound of their redemption charging towards them.

"Here I go..." Zane said, not realising that the quiver in his voice would reveal just how terrified he was.

"Here *we* go." Astrid reached across from her seat and placed her supple hand onto his.

For a glorious, fleeting moment, they had been human. And that was enough. Together, they decided that the day the transcendent were born did not have to be the beginning of another self-destructive cycle.

It could also be the end.

Printed in Great Britain
by Amazon